BEARISTA

BODYGUARD SHIFTERS #1

ZOE CHANT

Bearista

Author's Note

This book stands alone and contains a complete HEA romance. However, if you'd like to read the other books in the Bodyguard Shifters series, here's the series so far, in order:

You may also enjoy Bodyguard Shifters Collection 1, collecting books 1-4.

GABY

Early morning shifts were the worst. Gaby Diaz tried to be quiet, tiptoeing around the dark apartment as she stuffed a piece of toast in the toaster, gathered up her clothes, tried to find her keys and transit card ... but then she stepped on a Lego, and it was all over.

"Ow ow ow! Fargin' bargin' muffin-biscuit frickety-frackety blarginfrack—" She let out a whispered string of fake swearing that would've done credit to a sailor—a sailor on the S.S. Lollipop, that is—all too aware of her five-year-old son and, worse, her mother in the next room. Clinging to the back of a chair, she massaged her foot until the string of fake swearing wound down with a muttered, heartfelt, "*Fudge!*"

When Gaby looked up, her mother was standing in the darkened doorway of the room she shared with Gaby's son Sandy. "Sorry, Mama," Gaby whispered. "I didn't mean to wake you up."

"Oh, no, I was already awake," her mother whispered back. She limped across the room to gather up the scattered toys and, along the way, paused to pick up Gaby's discarded cardigan and neatly fold it. She was recovering from hip surgery, but still tried to keep the place clean, always a chore with Hurricane Sandy running around all day. "If you have the 4:30 a.m. shift at the coffee shop this morning, you'll be home in early afternoon, won't you? That's nice; you and Sandy can go to the park before your evening classes. It'll do him good to get outside."

Gaby's heart twinged. "I'm sorry, Mama. I'm covering a shift for one of my co-workers this afternoon so I can pick up some overtime. But," she added, "I don't have classes tonight, so I'll be home for dinner. I can pick up something nice if I get good tips. Maybe I'll get some beef so you can make your world-famous carne guisada tomorrow."

Luisa Diaz kissed her daughter's cheek. "A girl your age should not work so hard. You need to find a nice man who will take care of you."

Yes, a man who'll take care of me and my entire family. That sounds likely. Not to mention, between all the overtime and the evening classes and being a full-time single mom, it's not like I have time for dating ...

"Well, let me know if you find one. Meanwhile—" She snatched up the folded cardigan and grabbed her shoes. "I'm going to miss my bus and be late for work. Love you!"

She hurried out the door, hopped on one foot as she pulled on her shoes, and was halfway down the stairs before she remembered that she'd forgotten her toast. Oh well, she could grab a bagel or a donut at work. The breakfast of champions ...

And she'd also forgotten the textbook she'd meant to take along to study for her accounting test during her commute. Gaby sighed and leaned her head against the window as the bus pulled away from her stop. Maybe she could take a nap instead.

She was so tired all the time. It felt like she was burning

her candle at both ends, trying to be a good mom and keep the family afloat while still planning for her future.

My mother's right. I sure could use a nice man. I don't know about taking care of me, but a second income wouldn't hurt. Not to mention the fringe benefits ...

She clamped her knees together and tried not to think about those fringe benefits, ones she hadn't enjoyed since breaking up with Sandy's deadbeat dad before her son was even born.

But unless the love of her life just happened to walk into the coffee shop, she was pretty much screwed—*or not screwed, that's the problem*—for the near future.

Oh well. Since she didn't have her textbook, she got out her phone, opened up a notepad app, and started making a shopping list for tonight. Napping could wait for a time in her life when she wasn't trying to support her family on minimum wage and earn a college degree.

But she did take a moment to twist her hair up and secure it with a clip so she didn't look quite so much like she'd just run down the street to catch a bus.

If Mr. Right picked today to walk into the coffee shop, at the very least she didn't want him to turn around in horror and walk right back out.

Gaby's stop was a few blocks down from the coffee shop, so she always had a bit of a walk. In the summer it wasn't bad, although for these morning shifts it was still dark, so she clutched her purse to her chest and walked swiftly.

As much as she hated having to drag herself out of bed for the 4:30 shift, especially when she'd been up late studying the night before, it was interesting to watch the city starting to wake up around her. The businesses were all still closed, except for an all-night convenience store on the corner, but delivery trucks were out and about. In little cafés and fast-food restaurants, some of the lights were on inside, sleepy-looking employees moving about as they prepared for the morning breakfast rush.

At the credit union a block down the street from the coffee shop, an armored car had pulled up onto the sidewalk, flashing its hazard lights while workers in brown uniforms swiftly unloaded it. Gaby paused to watch; she'd never seen that much money in one place before. At least, that's what she guessed was in those deceptively small canvas bags. One guy stood in the back of the truck and tossed the bags to his co-worker, who was—

—tossing the bags into the open door of the large black sedan parked on the curb behind the armored car.

... wait a minute.

Just as Gaby realized that she wasn't looking at a delivery but a robbery, the guy catching the bags looked up, straight across the street, at her.

Gaby's brain stuttered in sheer panic.

He was a huge guy with a blond crew cut and ice-pale eyes, pale enough to startle her even from across the street, lit only by the street lights and the growing light of dawn in the sky. And that bulge under his jacket *definitely* didn't mean he was happy to see her.

The guy tossing the bags realized his catching buddy wasn't catching anymore, and now they were both looking at her. Bag-Toss Guy dropped his bag and reached under his jacket.

Gaby turned and ran.

There was nothing open on the whole street. The coffee shop was the nearest place to go, but she would have to stop and unlock the door. Instead, she ducked down the alley behind the row of shops. Usually the coffee shop's owner and chief baker, Polly, would already be at work, which meant the back door would be unlocked and Gaby could get in without having to stop and fumble with her keys.

She heard pounding feet and a shout behind her. In the darkness of the alley, she stumbled into a garbage can, and despite knowing she had to run, she couldn't resist looking back.

The big guy with the pale eyes was framed in the entrance to the alley; she recognized him by his hulking size and the halo-like glow of the street light on his blond hair. He tore off his jacket and flung it aside. Underneath, he wore a gun, but he wasn't drawing it. Instead he leaned over and—

Gaby stared.

His big shoulders humped up enormously. His shirt tore off. And as he leaned forward, it wasn't human hands that thumped to the pavement, but the massive front paws of a —*polar bear?*

A tiny squeak of terror escaped her. The bear's huge head went up, covered in fur so white it seemed to glow.

Gaby was afraid to take her eyes off him. She stumbled backward, groping at the wall, trying to find the door to the coffee shop. Her hands closed on the familiar metal handle that she opened a dozen times a day. It was unlocked—*Oh, thank you, Polly.* Gaby tore it open and stumbled into the kitchen, slamming it behind her and throwing the deadbolt.

The kitchen was brightly lit, and Polly, a big woman with masses of curly hair pulled back in a hairnet, stared at Gaby over the rows and rows of baking sheets she was laying out. The warm air in the kitchen was fragrant with cinnamon and hot grease.

"Hon? You okay?"

"No," Gaby gasped. "We need to call the police. I—I just—"

And then she stopped, because she could hear, on the

other side of the door, the sound of snuffling and the shuffling of big paws.

Gaby scrambled away from the door, grabbed Polly's arm, and pulled her out of the kitchen.

"Where are we—"

"Shhhh!" Gaby pulled her down behind the counter and tried to get her phone out, but her hands were shaking so hard she dropped her purse, spilling its contents on the floor behind the coffee-shop counter. All the lights were still off in the main part of the shop, but she didn't feel safe at all, not with those huge picture windows looking out at the darkened street. A bear could smash through those in an instant. "Call the police. There's a robbery happening at the credit union, right now."

Polly didn't panic or argue, just pulled out her phone with a plastic-gloved, floury hand and started dialing.

Gaby crawled along the counter and peeked back into the kitchen. It looked just as they'd left it, just as it looked every morning. It didn't seem like the bear had tried to break in after her.

But it knew where she had gone.

A moment later, she heard the wailing of sirens. Gaby screwed up her courage enough to tiptoe through the darkened coffee shop to peek out the window, looking down the street.

The armored car was still there, but the dark sedan behind it had gone. Flashing red and blue lights were visible at the end of the street, and a moment later, police cars pulled up onto the sidewalk.

Polly joined her, putting an arm around her shoulders. "Oh, hon. You're shaking like a leaf. What an awful thing to see. You must be terrified."

More than you know. Had she really just seen a man turn

into a bear? How could she tell the police the truth? They were going to think she was nuts.

But she *had* to tell them. If she didn't, they were going to get killed when they tried to arrest him.

And he'd seen her. He'd *smelled* her. He knew which door she'd fled through. He could come back and find her anytime he wanted.

Clinging to Polly, Gaby burst into tears.

DEREK

Derek Ruger was already up when his phone vibrated to indicate an incoming call. He'd just come in from his morning run and was toweling off. The run had helped settle his thoughts and his bear after the nightmares that had jolted him awake a couple of hours earlier.

He rarely slept through the night, but last night had been unusually bad. He was still tense, even after running until his muscles ached. At least his bear was no longer clawing up the wallpaper of his soul.

And now this. Derek grimaced at the sight of Lt. Keegan's number on his screen and thought about just going back to bed. His old friend never called just to say hi. With a sigh, he picked up the call.

"We had a shifter-related incident this morning," Keegan said, not bothering with pleasantries.

"Hello to you too." Derek reached for the coffeepot and dumping out the dregs into the sink. "One of these days we could just get drinks or catch a game on TV. But no, it's always work, work, work—"

"The Ghost might be involved."

That got Derek's attention—and his bear's attention, too. He could feel the grizzly inside him bristling, its ears going flat and its hackles standing up. He stood frozen with the coffeepot in his hand, and for an instant he was back in the mountains, with the giant polar bear stalking him, its claws tearing into him—

Water spilled over his hand, jolting him back to himself. He cursed under his breath.

"Ruger?" Keegan said. "You there?"

"So the Ghost's in town," Derek said harshly. Maybe that was what had riled up his bear.

"Unless it's some other enormous polar bear shifter. But we have a witness who ID'd him from a photograph."

Derek set the coffeepot down and leaned on the edge of the sink. Shit just had a way of following him home. "What'd he do this time?"

"Robbed an armed car, with an accomplice."

"Really? That doesn't sound like his style. Guess working as an assassin for gangsters and warlords doesn't pay so well anymore."

"Solving the crime is our end," Keegan said. His voice dropped slightly. "Here's why I'm calling you. The witness, Gabriella Diaz, saw him shift. And he also saw her."

"So he'll be coming after her," Derek said softly.

"Almost certainly. I'd put a regular protection detail on her, but we're stretched pretty thin and anyway, putting a human cop up against the Ghost would be like slapping a bandaid on a spillway during a flood. Nothing against my guys and gals, but he'd go right through them. You still do private security work sometimes, right?"

"Right." Despite the pressure of the bear snarling in his chest, Derek had to grin. Keegan might be a cop now, and he might be a badass panther shifter, but he actually had an engineering degree. It was always a little disconcerting to hear construction metaphors dropping out of his mouth.

They'd met in South America when Derek was working for an international security company and Keegan was scouting dam locations for a development firm. And because Keegan had known him then, Keegan also knew what had happened the last time Derek tangled with the Ghost.

Right now his bear was in full battle mode, itching for a rematch with that polar-bear-shifting asshole.

"We're not going to be able to pay you," Keegan said. "At least not much."

"Forget the money. I'm willing to do this as a favor to you. I probably owe you a lot more than that. And anyway—" Derek could feel his bear inside him, straining to come out. "—I definitely owe the Ghost a thing or two."

"Yeah, well, just remember your first priority is the witness. Miss Diaz is at a coffee shop on Fifth called the Daily Bean. Good luck with it."

Derek parked on the street outside the coffee shop. The city was starting to wake up around him, businesses opening up and commuters going to work. Just down the street, police cars and uniformed officers were clustered around the armored car parked in front of the credit union.

Derek went to the armored car first. The witness could wait. He needed to get a good sniff before the forensic team trampled all over everything, if it wasn't already too late. One whiff of the perp's scent would tell him whether he was really dealing with Ghost or not.

A uniformed cop stepped into his path, giving him a distrusting look. Derek knew he wasn't the most reputable-looking person, with a beat-up leather jacket flung over his T-shirt. "Buddy, this is a restricted area," the cop told him, and nodded to the gun on Derek's hip. "You got a permit for that?"

"I sure as hell do. Give Lieutenant Keegan a call. I'm doing some consulting for him."

Just then he caught sight of Keegan on the far side of the armored car, talking to the police photographer. Keegan noticed him too, raised a hand in greeting, and loped over.

The lieutenant was slim and dark, giving off an air of barely contained danger. He'd had that even back when he was an engineer; now that he was a cop, it was honed like a blade. "I don't remember inviting you to stomp around my crime scene, Ruger. The witness is at the coffee shop."

"I need to check something." Derek touched his nose. Keegan was a shifter; he'd understand. "Where were the suspects when the witness saw them?"

He saw comprehension flicker on Keegan's face. "Back of the armored car. There was a getaway car back there too, but it's gone now."

Derek's sense of smell wasn't nearly as sharp in human form as if he'd been able to shift, but he leaned close to the open back door of the armored car, getting a curious glance from the forensic tech who was dusting for prints. There were a lot of overlapping smells back here, but there was also a faint, elusive trace that he'd last smelled in the Andes Mountains, years ago.

Inside him, his bear uncoiled in fury, a thousand-pound killing machine gearing up for action.

He's here!

"Ghost?" Keegan asked, very softly.

"Ghost." It emerged as a low growl.

Keegan's hand closed over Derek's arm. His fingers were strong as steel. "Keep your mind in the game," the lieutenant said quietly. "Your job is to protect the witness. This isn't about revenge."

Derek took a slow breath, pushing down his bear and his temper. The scars on his side seemed to pulse with a sudden memory of pain. "I'm not gonna do anything crazy," he said, as much to his bear as to Keegan.

Keegan released him, and Derek strode up the street, his bear straining on its inner leash. His bear wanted to go to the witness as badly as it wanted to take down the Ghost, which was a surprise. Maybe the bear knew that where the witness was, Ghost was likely to follow.

Derek paused outside the coffee shop. There was an OPEN sign hanging in the window, and a few people carrying cups of coffee and paper bags of pastries brushed past him as he hesitated. He'd never actually been inside a place like this before. Five-dollar coffee drinks with whipped cream on top and pumpkin spice pastries with sprinkles *really* weren't his style. He liked his coffee strong and black, and his donuts four for a dollar, and the only thing he wanted to find pumpkin spices inside was a pumpkin pie.

Aren't we going in? his bear wanted to know. It was unaccountably antsy for some reason.

Yeah, yeah. Keep your fur on.

A little bell tinkled on the door as he opened it. *Of course* this was the kind of place that had a tinkly little bell. Derek stepped inside and looked around.

Most of the customers were at the counter, but his attention went immediately to the black-haired woman sitting at a table, talking to a uniformed police officer.

She was riveting. Glorious raven waves of hair swept back like wings from a cute face with a snub nose, full lips, and a splattering of freckles a few shades darker than her light brown skin. Her generous, curvy figure filled the khaki-colored Daily Bean T-shirt she was wearing; a purple cardigan thrown over the top of it accentuated rather than hid her curves.

Inside him, his bear went suddenly on high alert, straining forward.

That's our mate. Our mate!

No wonder his bear had wanted to get to the coffee shop so damn bad. No wonder it had been tense and weird for the last few days.

It just freakin' figured. He'd never really been sure if he believed in fated mates and all that stuff his Gran used to talk about. And now, here he was, with his past coming back to haunt him—and this *would* be the time when his mate would enter the picture, because fate liked to dump on him.

So much for any chance of this not getting personal.

He understood now what Gran had been talking about. *You'll know it when it happens*, she'd said, and he sure as hell did. It was like a bolt of lightning between the eyes. He had to struggle to pull himself together before he crossed the room, weaving his way between little café-style tables and tiny chairs that looked too flimsy to hold him without collapsing under his weight.

Everything about this place made him feel big and clumsy, especially as he stood over the little table where the curvy brunette was sitting and looking perfectly at home, her small brown hands wrapped around a mug with a curl of whipped cream on top of it.

"I'm here to protect her," Derek said. "Keegan sent me."

The uniformed cop nodded. "The Lieutenant said you were coming." He got up hastily. Humans weren't as sensitive to shifter dominance hierarchies as shifters themselves, but Derek had noticed in the past that humans often responded instinctively to shifters, especially to the big animals, bears and wolves and cats. It was useful in his line of work;

humans didn't exactly fear him, but they sensed the air of danger around him.

And right now, he was a shifter whose bear was giving off a powerful vibe of *You are sitting in my mate's space. Get out of it.*

Knock it off, asshole, Derek told his bear, though he was having to squash down the feeling himself. *He's just doing his job.*

And then his mate looked up at him, and he was almost knocked off his feet by her eyes: soft brown, with hints of green and gray. *She* wasn't afraid of him. He could see it in her face, in the glorious depths of those summer-forest eyes. Most humans pulled away from him, not even understanding why; their subconscious instincts knew what their conscious minds did not.

But his mate didn't even have a shred of fear, not for the big man looming over her table, and not for the bear inside him. In fact, she was looking at him with an expression as stunned as Derek must have looked, when he'd walked in and first caught sight of her.

She feels it too! his bear rumbled, pleased.

And then his mate seemed to shake herself back to reality. "I—I'm sorry. I'm Gaby Diaz, but I guess you probably know that, if you're here to protect me. I didn't catch your name?"

"Derek Ruger." He held out a hand; her small fingers vanished into his big, gun-callused ones. Her skin felt so soft. He had to make himself let go. "Like I said, I'm here to protect you." He pulled out one of the flimsy-looking little chairs and sat in it carefully, his knees bumping the bottom of the table.

"Oh. Good." She looked pleased by that, the corners of her lips turning up before she visibly forced them down.

Up close, Derek could see the traces of dried tears on her

face. His bear bristled inside him, wanting to rip the fur off that bastard who'd scared her this much.

"Are you a police officer?" she asked him.

"No. Private security."

She touched her fingers to her lips. Derek tried not to follow the movement of her hand—tried not to think about how very soft and touchable her lips looked. "That's not usual, is it?" she said.

"No. It's an unusual situation. Lieutenant Keegan—you met him, right? Dark hair with a little gray, looks like he's made of all sharp edges?" This brought out a little grin, and she nodded. "He's an old friend. We've worked together in the past. You can call him if you're not sure about me."

"That's fine," she said. "I trust you."

So soft. So trusting. What must it be like to live in a world like that? Although from the look on her face, that soft world of trusted authority figures had been blown apart this morning.

"The lieutenant filled me in on what you saw at the credit union."

Her brown eyes with their half-hidden depths searched his face. Derek had to fight down a powerful urge to reach out and brush his fingertips across the soft curve of her cheek. "Did—did he tell you *everything* I saw?"

"You saw a man turn into a bear," Derek said quietly.

She gave a short, jerky nod. "No one seems to believe me. I couldn't tell if the lieutenant believed me, but at least he didn't look at me like I was crazy."

"He believed you," Derek said softly. "And so do I."

Her eyes went wide, and she gazed at him for a long, quiet moment. "You do."

"I do," he said. It hovered on the tip of his tongue to tell her *why* he believed her, but he couldn't quite make the words come out. She'd only just found out that shifters existed. Telling her that the cop who was protecting her was also a shifter, and a bear on top of that, didn't seem like the best idea right now.

She's going to find out eventually, his bear grumbled.

Eventually, sure. Not while she's still shaken up from having the Ghost chase her!

"Is that ... a thing that can happen, then?" she asked, clasping the mug in her hands. Derek started to lift a hand to place it over hers, but forced it back down on the table.

She's human. And she's in your care right now. Don't move too fast or tell her too much too soon. Don't scare her off.

"It's not common. The people who can do it are called shifters." He glanced around to make sure that no one was near enough to overhear, but she was at a table in the very corner, and the cheerful buzz of morning coffee-shop conversation covered their quiet voices.

"Yeah, that's what the lieutenant said." She looked down at her cup, then up at him again, quickly. "He also said the man I saw, the, uh, the polar bear, is very dangerous."

"He is. He's called the Ghost. And trust me, you don't want to go up against him. I've done it. I barely got out alive."

A swift intake of breath between her full lips. "You *know* him?"

"We're not friends, if that's what you're thinking."

Now she was looking at him with a narrow-eyed, suspicious stare. "Next you're going to tell me *you* can turn into a bear."

Derek was too caught off guard to answer immediately.

"Holy sh—*Do* you turn into a bear?"

"Well, it makes sense, doesn't it?" Derek asked quietly. "Send a bear to catch a bear."

And now he couldn't help wondering if Keegan had somehow *known* she was his mate—but no, that wasn't the sort of thing any shifter could tell about another one.

He'd been drawn here because she was his destiny. If it hadn't been this, it would have been a chance meeting some other day. His Gran had said you couldn't escape it. If you were meant for each other, you would be drawn to each other, no matter what.

"I don't know whether to believe you or not."

"I can prove it to you somewhere else," Derek told her. "And right now, somewhere else is where you need to go. You're not safe here. I'll take you to a place where you will be. We can stop by your home to pick up some things."

Gaby shook her head. "I can't."

"What do you mean, you can't?"

"Like I told the lieutenant, I can't just drop everything and run off to a—a safehouse or whatever. I have a job. Family. Responsibilities." She glanced guiltily toward the counter. "I should be helping Polly with the morning rush right now."

"Your job isn't more important than your life," Derek said.

"Now listen, Mr. Ruger—"

"This might be easier if you call me Derek."

"—*Mr. Ruger*, I'm going to school and supporting my family. I can't just put my entire life on hold."

"Even if someone very dangerous is after you." This woman's stubbornness and fire was a huge turn-on. She might not be a shifter, but she had a bear's soul, brave and strong and protective.

Too bad it was so damned inconvenient right now.

And it didn't help that all he wanted to do was pull her into his arms so he could explore her generous curves with his hands and lips—

Down, boy!

"Yes," she said firmly. "Look, I know your job is to keep me safe. Believe me, I want me to be safe too, for my son's sake as well as my own. But—"

Son? Derek and his bear thought, startled.

She was his mate. So clearly she didn't have another mate already. And yet. *Son?*

"—but it's also because of my son that I can't just throw away my job and my future. Not even if this Ghost person is after me."

"You can get another job," Derek said. "You can't get another life."

"Can't you protect me here? If I'd be safe in a hotel room or a safehouse, wouldn't I be just as safe in the coffee shop if you're here?" A tiny crease appeared between her brows as she looked at him. "I—I know it doesn't make any sense, but I already feel safer just because you're here. I don't know why."

Of course she felt safer with her mate here to protect her. Even if her newfound confidence was a damned nuisance for him. "It's not a secure location," Derek said. "There are windows, multiple entrances, people coming and going all the time." He glanced up, just in time to see the woman behind the counter vanish into the back and reappear with a tray of donuts in her oven-mitted hands. "And I can't keep an eye on you properly if you're at the counter and I'm over here. Someone could move in on you when you're out of my sight."

"So what if you were behind the counter with me?" she suggested. "Like, undercover? You can do that kind of thing, right?"

"Sure, but in case you hadn't noticed, I'm not exactly inconspicuous." He gestured a hand to indicate the whole, big, six-foot-five expanse of himself, noting the way Gaby's eyes followed his gesture up and down his body. He might pass for human, but there was no way to hide the body-builder's shoulders, the tattoos peeking out from under the sleeves of his T-shirt, the rugged jaw and tense, alert fighter's stance.

He was used to being muscle for hire, whether as private

security or a bouncer or the various other things he'd done since coming back to the States, scarred in body and soul. Looking intimidating was part of his profession.

But it didn't exactly help him fit in at a coffee shop.

"Look, that's the deal," Gaby said, folding her arms, though her gaze lingered on his chest under the shirt. "Just let me get through today's shift, and then we can work out what to do next, okay? I'll explain to my boss. She saw how scared I was this morning. I don't think she'll mind if you stick around. It's like having security for the whole café, in a way."

He couldn't understand how this conversation had spun so completely out of his control. "Miss—er, Mrs. Diaz—" His whole body cringed from using the married honorific, especially the bear inside him. *Mate!*

But—she'd said *son*—

She wasn't wearing a ring, though.

"It's Miss—well, Ms., actually," Gaby said. Her eyes flashed in challenge. "Okay, so you don't like my idea. If you'd rather, you can sit over here and nurse a latte while I pull coffee shots. You won't be *that* far away."

"Too far away if the Ghost shows up," Derek said with finality.

"You'll do it, then?" Despite the tear tracks on her face and her obvious weariness, a glimmer of humor sparked in her eyes.

"I'll do it," Derek said, and wondered whether Keegan was going to laugh or cry when he explained the situation.

GABY

During a lull between customers, Gaby went into the kitchen to talk to Polly.

"Well, that's certainly a prime hunk of manflesh you were talking to over there," were the first words out of Polly's mouth.

"You only think that because you haven't had to talk to him," Gaby said, firmly stomping on the part of her that agreed a hundred percent.

He *had* to have been making fun of her with the crack about turning into a bear—hadn't he?

You saw that other guy turn into a bear—

Maybe she'd lost her mind completely. That would explain everything: why she was seeing people transform into animals, why she couldn't even sit at the same table with frustrating, annoyingly muscle-bound Derek Ruger without wanting to climb all over him—

"Well, if you don't want him ..." Polly grinned.

Gaby blushed all the way to her hairline. "Aren't you married?"

"Seventeen years and counting, but that doesn't mean I can't look. Who is he? Police?"

"No—well, yes, sort of. He's not a detective, but the police sent him to protect me. They're afraid the thieves might come back looking for me. I'm so, so sorry about all of this."

"Not your fault, hon. Hand me that measuring cup there, would you?"

Gaby passed the requested item across the countertop. "I was just about to get back to work, but Der—uh—Mr. Ruger is going to stick around today, if that's okay?"

"If there's any chance of those men you saw coming back to bother you, I'd much rather have him here. And ..." Polly waggled her eyebrows at Gaby. "It'll give us a nice view, won't it?"

Gaby's cheeks felt hot enough to toast bread on. Those shoulders, that chest—*aargh*. What was wrong with her? She'd never reacted to another man with anything approaching this intensity before, not even Sandy's dad. *Especially* not Sandy's dad.

"How about a closer view?" she asked hopefully, and then winced as the thought shot straight to her libido. "I mean! Behind the counter! I was wondering if Mr. Ruger could pretend to be a barista for a day, so he could stay closer to me. He's worried that he won't be close enough if there's trouble."

"Does he know how to do the job?"

"No," Gaby admitted. "But I can train him. I've trained new people before."

"You don't even really have to do that, I suppose, as long as he stays out of the way and we don't trip over him." Polly raised her brows again. "Though I wouldn't mind tripping over him, if you know what I mean."

Gaby covered her face with her hands. This was even more embarrassing than having her mother trying to micromanage her dating life. "So it's okay?" she asked, peeking out between her fingers.

"It's fine, honey. Just make sure he doesn't do anything to violate health codes or annoy the customers."

"I promise there won't be any problems. I'll keep a short leash on him." Gaby floundered. "I mean—"

"Settle down and get back out there. Looks like we've got a line at the counter."

They did have a line. Gaby hurried to attend to the customers, all the while very aware of Derek sitting at the table in the back, watching her with his dark, level gaze. He was so *intense*. She could feel his eyes on her even when she turned away to throw together a breakfast burrito for the next customer, as if there was a magnetic connection between the two of them, holding them together even when they were apart.

What is going on here? First men who turned into bears, then an enormous, tatted-out security guard who made her weak in the knees.

It's like my life has turned into one of those romance novels I used to read, back when I had time to read for fun ...

She handed the breakfast burrito across the counter and ran the customer's credit card. That was the last one, so she made a "come here" gesture at Derek, who got up and sauntered over as the customer left.

He even *walked* sexy, a casually confident leonine prowl that made something in her hindbrain perk up to attention. As Derek leaned on the counter, Gaby had the sudden realization that letting him back here with her meant that she was going to have to spend the whole day in close proximity to him. *Very* close proximity. There was just barely room behind the counter for two people to move around, as long as they didn't mind bumping into each other occasionally.

She could think of some parts of him she'd *love* to bump into ...

Gaby cleared her throat and tried to pretend she wasn't blushing like a sunrise. "My boss said it's all right, so congratulations, Derek Ruger. You get to be a barista for a day."

The look on Derek's face said that he was starting to rethink this plan. "I'm not sure if I like calling myself a barista—"

"Well, too bad, because it's your official job title now." She pointed to a rack on the wall containing khaki T-shirts with the coffee shop logo. "See if there's something in your size hanging there. You'll need to wear it while you're back here."

For a moment she thought he wasn't going to. Then he smiled (her knees wobbled again), and she got an amazing rear view of his tight ass and rippling shoulder muscles as he strolled with that casual, confident stride over to the T-shirt rack and picked one out.

"You can change in the storeroom," Gaby said, trying very hard not to think about all the manflesh—to use Polly's term —that would shortly be on display among their stored cases of paper towels and coffee beans.

The bell on the coffee shop's front door tinkled to announce the departure of the last customer who'd been seated at the tables. With the breakfast rush winding down and the lunch crowd not yet ramping up, the Daily Bean was now empty. Derek gave Gaby a sudden, quick, panty-melting grin.

"Long as I'm quick, it should be okay to change here, right?"

Her mouth dropped open. "Uh ..."

Derek didn't wait, just stripped quickly out of the white T-shirt he was wearing, and any attempt at rational thought went up, *poof!*, in a bombardment of muscles! and tattoos! and flexing! and ... wow ...

Then he turned and she saw the scars on his side. Her breath caught in her throat. Pale, parallel scars, wrapping all the way around his ribs and across his stomach. Like someone had tried to disembowel him with a parallel set of knives.

Claws, some part of her brain told her. *Those are claw marks.*

And the way he was looking at her as he pulled on the T-shirt was not just flirtatious, it was challenging. He *wanted* her to see this.

Did—did the Ghost do that?

He's trying to make me change my mind. He wants me to know what I'm up against.

Well, if this was the game he wanted to play, then she'd play it right back. Instead of looking at the scars, she flicked her gaze up to his face, and touched the tip of her tongue to her lips. Lasciviously, she let her gaze trail down his pecs and the flat muscles of his abdomen.

The hair on his head was buzzed off too short to be sure of the color, but his chest hair was a medium brown, curling gently across those incredible pecs. Gaby's covetous gaze followed his treasure trail down to the waistband of his jeans, where the belt for his gun holster was slung low across his narrow hips—

—and then it all vanished under a Daily Bean T-shirt. The chest of the shirt, like Gaby's, was printed with the cup-and-coffee-beans shop logo. Gaby couldn't help thinking that those were some very lucky coffee beans.

"Holy Mary Mother of God," Polly murmured behind Gaby.

Gaby's reaction astonished her: a sudden, intense surge of territoriality. *Mine!* she wanted to snarl, whirling around on the older woman.

She got control of herself almost immediately. Derek

wasn't hers! He was just a security guard who was protecting her. Nothing more.

But she could feel right down to her bones (and other parts of her), as Derek sauntered back to the counter, that he wasn't "just" anything. This was the kind of man who slammed into your life like a freight train. Nothing would ever be the same again.

.... a man like Sandy's father?

No! cried one part of her, but it was overruled by the cautious part of her—the part that had *learned* to be cautious, after getting burned so badly by a charming asshole who'd waltzed off and never wanted a thing to do with the son he'd left her.

She was *not* getting close. She was *not* falling again.

Firmly she pushed down her feelings beneath a cool, professional veneer.

This got harder when Derek came around the end of the counter and suddenly it felt much, *much* too small back here. She wasn't even going to be able to turn around without bouncing off him.

Why did I suggest this?

Why did I ever think this was a good idea?

"What do I do first, ma'am?" he asked, smiling down at her. She hadn't realized he was so incredibly tall. The top of her head didn't even come up to his chin. She was on eyeball level with his chest, and the T-shirt straining across his pecs. It looked like she could've bounced a quarter off those coffee beans.

Sandy's father was tall too, she reminded herself. *Be cool! Be professional!*

She also tried to remember that Polly was standing right there, and the last thing she wanted to do was rub her face all over Derek's pecs in front of her boss.

"What do you want me to show him first?" she asked

Polly, taking a step back so she wasn't standing *quite* so close to Derek and all his tantalizing ... everything.

"I don't suppose you have the first clue how to make a proper cup of coffee, do you?" Polly asked him.

"Sure I can. Just give me the coffeemaker and the can of roast."

Polly winced. "I'm going to say that's a 'no.' Why don't we put those muscles to some use, and have you start by taking the trash out."

Derek glanced at Gaby. "She'll have to come with me. I'm not leaving her unattended out here."

"Oh, for Pete's sake!" Gaby exclaimed, causing the couple who had just entered the coffee shop to jump back in a clash of tinkling bells. "Is this what it's going to be like all day? You don't have to be glued to my hip every waking minute!"

Derek leaned forward, into her space, so close his breath tickled her hair. "Yeah, I do," he said quietly. "If you won't do this my way and go to a safe place, then I'm gonna stick to you like glue. You don't know what this guy is like. I do. I'm not leaving you alone for a minute."

Gaby gulped. He was so ... *close* ...

She could smell his spicy male scent, mingled with the scents of cinnamon and coffee.

If her control lapsed for an instant, she could lean forward and touch the five o'clock shadow already prickling his jaw—brush her lips across his too-near mouth—

Gaby took a hasty step away, reclaiming some space and also some self-control. "Okay, fine. Stick with me like glue, I don't care. I really couldn't care less what you do," she lied.

"If you're going back to the kitchen, you could bring out a fresh batch of donuts," Polly suggested. "And see if the calzones are cool enough to put out on the rack. I'll handle the customers."

Feeling a little better with some sense of purpose, Gaby

went into the kitchen with Derek at her side. She obstinately did not look at him, which made her aware of how very silently he moved. How could such a big man be so silent? He was like a ghost himself.

Maybe he was *serious about being able to turn into a bear ...*

And it was true that she did feel much safer with him around. Being in the kitchen brought it all back: the sound of snuffling outside the door, the awareness that a giant predator was right on the other side—

"You okay?" Derek asked quietly, and she realized she'd stopped, staring at the door.

"I'm fine." She pointed to the trash bags beside the door. "Those go out in the bin in the alley. That's, uh, that's where the Ghost was, so I'll just be over here at the calzones, if you don't mind."

When she looked up from using a pair of tongs to take the calzones off the rack, she saw that Derek had drawn his gun from the holster at his waist. "Stay back there," he told her, and opened the door, looking out into the alley.

"Do you think he's still there?" Her voice rose in a squeak of nervousness.

"Just making sure he's not." Derek holstered the gun. "Come here."

"Why?" Gaby asked, but she put the tongs down and came over to the door. Even with Derek there, she had to nerve herself to step out into the alley. It was obvious at a glance that they were alone, though.

"I'm guessing this wasn't here before," Derek said. He pointed to the bricks beside the door.

Gaby looked, and swallowed. Fresh scrapes gleamed in the soot-stained brick, four parallel marks beside the door, as if a huge paw with claws like scimitars had scraped it.

She couldn't help noticing that the marks were just about the size of the scars on Derek's side.

"He tried to claw his way in," she said in a faint voice.

"If he'd *really* been trying to get in, he probably could have," Derek said. "He's just marking the door so he can come back later. *Now* do you believe me that you need to get somewhere safe?"

Gaby balled her hands into fists. "You still don't get it, do you? It's not that I'm not afraid. I know this guy is dangerous. But I *need* this paycheck. I'm a single mom trying to support my kid and my widowed, disabled mother. I can't just disappear. We've barely got enough people to run the coffee shop as it is. Polly would have to hire someone to replace me, and I *get* that, but—look, you're only going to be in my life as long as the Ghost is after me. But I'm still going to have to live my life after you're gone, including paying my rent and my tuition and my grocery bill, okay?"

Derek gazed at her for a moment before he murmured, "Stubborn woman."

He sounded admiring.

"So we'll stay here, right?" she said, folding her arms. "You'll protect me here?"

A smile quirked up the corner of his mouth. "Yes, I'll protect you here."

DEREK

He'd stay here with her, if this was where she wanted to be. Derek was willing to be wherever Gaby wanted to be.

But being this close to his mate, not being able to touch her, was torment.

In the narrow space behind the counter, it was impossible not to brush against her constantly. Every time one of them turned around, those sweet curves were sliding past him, her round hip bumping against his.

It didn't take long before he was fighting down a raging hard-on.

Gaby showed him how to use the cash register and process credit cards. "Probably better if you stay out of the kitchen as much as possible. That's Polly's domain, and she's very particular about it. Why don't you handle the next customer? It looks like she's ready to order. I'll make the drinks."

He couldn't believe was doing this, he really couldn't —"Hello, ma'am," Derek said with his most winning smile. "What can I get for you?"

"Well, *hello* there." The woman gave him a long, appraising once-over, lingering on his chest and on the tats peeking out from under the sleeves of his Daily Bean T-shirt. "You must be new. I think I'd remember *you*."

Behind the coffee machine, Gaby scowled.

Derek wasn't quite sure how to react, between his mate's flattering yet utterly misplaced jealousy and the customer who was looking at him like a prime slab of beef in a meat market. "I'm new here," he said. "Just started today."

The woman leaned on the counter. "I know where I'm getting *my* coffee from now on."

Gaby wiped down the coffee machine with needlessly brisk strokes of a damp rag, her expression murderous.

Derek cleared his throat. "And ... what did you want?"

"Oh, I think I'd like a *tall* latte ..." Her gaze ran up and down his body; now he knew what "undressed me with their eyes" meant. "—*extra* strong, with a shot of ..." Now she was attempting to gaze into his eyes. "—hazelnut."

Derek tried not to encourage her by making eye contact; he stared at a point over her shoulder instead. "Got that?" he asked Gaby.

"I've definitely got it," Gaby said in a strangled voice.

Derek watched out of the corner of his eye to make sure Gaby didn't spit in the drink, but she was perfectly professional.

The woman stuffed a $10 bill in the tip cup before she left, drink in hand, with several longing looks back.

"The nerve of her," Gaby muttered. Then she noticed Derek looking at her and cleared her throat. "I mean ... you're an employee. Just doing your job. The way she was objectifying you! How very ... inappropriate."

She didn't look at his pecs once throughout that entire speech, just kept her eyes fixed firmly on his face.

Our mate is fierce! his bear said approvingly.

She certainly was. Derek hoped they could get through the entire day without his fierce mate flinging herself across the counter to take down the next woman who looked at him that way.

She feels it too! She wants us; we can smell it. Why don't we just take our mate out into the forest and find a nice patch of grass—

Because it's more complicated for people, Derek thought at his bear, *and besides, we're in the city, so forest is hard to find. I'm not making love to my mate for the first time in a public park.*

Oh really? his libido contributed to the conversation, perking up.

No one asked you!

There was a steady stream of customers after that, which at least kept him busy enough to distract him (sort of) from Gaby's tempting curves right next to him. A suspicious number of the customers were young women. It seemed that word was getting around.

If looks could kill, Gaby's death glares would have left smoking craters on the floor.

On the bright side, the tip jar was filling up fast.

"You know, I have an idea," Gaby said when the last customer left and they had a few moments of peace again. "Why don't *you* make the coffee and *I'll* hold down the counter."

"Yeah, but—" Derek hesitated at admitting that he didn't know how to run the machine. He'd brought down drug dealers! He'd rescued kidnapping victims! He could hold his own in a firefight or a South American jungle.

He should not be brought low by a machine that made overpriced coffee drinks.

Still—all those *nozzles*—

His bear didn't like it either.

"Come here," Gaby sighed. She pointed out the different

parts of the machine, showed him how to turn the steam nozzle on and off, and how to run the coffee grinder. "Why don't you start out by making me a latte."

We can provide nourishment for our mate! His bear approved.

"That's the one with coffee and hot milk, right?"

"Right," Gaby agreed.

"Why not *say* 'coffee and milk'? It doesn't need a fancy name. Lots of people put milk in coffee."

"Because—it—look, just ..." She slapped the coffee-containing device (a small metal cup with a spigot, on a handle) into his palm. "This is a portafilter. It holds two shots of espresso. Fill it up at the grinder, tamp it down with this —" She put a little mallet in his other hand. "And lock it onto the machine. Okay? I'll get the milk."

The milk was kept in a little fridge underneath the counter. To get it, she had to bend over, giving him an excellent view of her firm, round behind ...

He wrenched his eyes away and tried to get his mind back on business. Coffee. Right.

Gaby straightened up with the jug of milk and set it on the counter. "Got the coffee? Okay, now you clamp the portafilter onto the machine—here—"

There was barely room for two of them at the machine. Gaby put her arms around him from behind, guiding his hand to clamp the portafilter into place. Her small, strong fingers wrapped around the back of his bigger hand—her curves pressed against him from behind—

"Like this?" he murmured.

"Like that." Her voice was throaty. Derek looked down as she peeled off him and ducked lithely under his arm, catching a glimpse of the blush tinting her tan cheek. She took a deep breath and her voice steadied. "You'll heat up the milk with the steam nozzle, in this pitcher here, while the hot water runs through the coffee into *this* little cup. The thermometer shows you when the milk's up to the right temperature. Don't let it get too hot, or it'll scald."

"I didn't think it would be this complicated," Derek admitted, dipping the head of the steam nozzle into the pitcher while the soft pressure of her hands guided him. "All the coffee I ever made, you just fill the pot. If you're camping, you boil it. No wonder these stu—er—these drinks are so expensive."

"Wait'll I get into making cappuccinos. For a latte, you just want a little bit of foam on top of the milk. Cappuccinos are all foam and they take a delicate touch. "

"I'm not so good at delicate," Derek said, his eyes not on the thermometer but on the small hands still covering his own.

"Oh, I don't know," Gaby murmured. "I bet you can be careful with those hands, when you want to be ..."

She blinked, made a tiny sound in her throat, and stepped back, the warmth of her hands and her body sliding away, leaving cold spots in their wake. She set a mug on the counter. "Your milk is almost hot enough. Coffee goes in first, then pour the milk after it, stirring as you go. Add a little dollop of foam on top, and you're done."

It smelled good, at least—the homey, enticing smell of hot coffee. Derek held the cup out to her. "Your latte, ma'am?"

Gaby smiled at him, dimpling adorably, and took the cup. She sipped. "Not bad. I declare this a passable latte."

"Only passable?"

"Well, it *is* your first one. Everybody improves after their first time."

In the limited space behind the counter, they were almost touching. She smelled like coffee and perfume and warm female skin.

"There are a few other things I'd like to improve on,"

Derek said quietly. "But to do that, we have to get to the first time."

She didn't step away. Head tipped back, lips parted—luscious, touchable lips. "Are we supposed to be doing this?" she asked on a breath.

"I'm not police," he whispered back. "I don't have any rules to follow. I won't tell if you won't."

Her lips—so near his own—

And then the doorbell tinkled and they took a quick, mutual step back. Derek bumped into the donut case; Gaby nearly dropped her latte.

The newcomer wasn't a customer. It was Lt. Keegan, dark and sharp in his black suit. "Ma'am," he said, nodding to Gaby, and jerked his head at Derek. "Ruger, a word."

Derek went to the corner table with him, glancing over his shoulder at Gaby, who watched with a look of concern.

"I see getting her to a safe place is going well," Keegan remarked, glancing at Derek's Daily Bean T-shirt.

"Protecting her here seemed preferable to throwing her over my shoulder and hauling her off to a safehouse by force," Derek said dryly. "People frown on that kind of thing these days."

"Noted," Keegan sighed.

"And there's another thing. You won't like it."

"Try me."

"She's my mate."

Keegan stared at him. Then he closed his eyes and rubbed at a crease between them. "Talk about a complication we don't need. I can guess what you'd say if I tried to pull you away now."

Derek's bear rose up with a rumbling growl. Derek shoved it down, but not all the way. "You're right about that." A hint of the growl lingered in his voice.

"Don't posture at me. I get it. In fact, as a fellow shifter, I get it better than anyone else could. Neither of you can stop it, and I know what'll happen to anyone who stands between you. But—" He leaned forward. "Be discreet, all right? At least as much as you're capable of. What I saw when I walked in wasn't discreet."

"I can be discreet."

"Uh-huh. Anyway," Keegan went on, "I came in to tell you, first of all, that we've sent a couple of uniforms around to keep an eye on her family. There's a kid and a grandma. The kid's dad doesn't seem to be in the picture."

Derek's stomach sank. He hadn't even considered that Gaby's family might be in danger. "Going after the family isn't the Ghost's usual M.O."

"I know that, but do you want to take chances with your mate's family?"

"No," Derek said, heartfelt.

"Didn't think so." Keegan slid a slip of paper across the table. "I've also reserved a hotel room where you can take her. Assuming you can get her to go there. Any sign of Ghost yet, by the way? Or ideas about where he might've gone to ground?"

Derek shook his head. "He was a merc, like me. He likes out-of-the-way places. I'm actually surprised to see him turn up in the city."

"Is there any chance he might be here *because* of you?"

"I doubt it." Derek grinned a fierce, feral grin with no humor in it. "I'm sure he wants a rematch as much as I do, but I don't see him following me all over the world just to get one. Our fight wasn't personal; it was part of the job."

Although it would be personal for *him* now. The Ghost had threatened his mate. His bear wouldn't let that kind of challenge pass unanswered.

"I still want to know why a guy like that is running around pulling ordinary robberies," Keegan said.

Derek's grin grew even fiercer, encouraged by his bear. "Let's find him and ask him, then."

"Yeah, well, we've got guys on that, so *you* get back up there and keep an eye on your mate." Keegan flashed one of his rare grins. "Congratulations on finding her, Derek. I know you've needed someone to settle you down for a while."

"So far, all she's done is get me riled up."

"Good. You need someone with a little fire in her." Keegan slapped him on the arm and got up to leave.

When Derek got back to the counter, Gaby asked, "What was all that about?"

"The lieutenant wanted to let me know they've reserved a hotel room—" *For us,* he almost said, realizing just in time that it could be taken the wrong way. "—for you to stay in until this is resolved."

"Why can't I just go home?" Then she clapped her hand over her mouth. "Mama! *Sandy!* Oh my God—"

She fumbled for her phone. Derek closed a hand over her wrist. "Your family is fine. There's a cop watching them."

Gaby jerked her wrist away. "I'm still calling them."

She stepped away with the phone to her ear. Derek watched her, feeling suddenly helpless—mainly because he couldn't protect both Gaby and her family at the same time, but also because of the reminder that she had a life apart from him.

Family. A son.

The kid's dad is out of the picture, Keegan said. What did that mean, anyway?

And what did it mean for Derek and Gaby?

For his bear, it was simple. They were mates. They had to be together.

But Gaby was human. She wouldn't look at it that way.

Is she married? Divorced?

She'd certainly been sending him active signals back. Clearly she was not with anyone else right now.

"Yes, Mama. I've got to get back to work. I'll tell you all about it this evening." She lowered the phone with a sigh. "They're all right."

"I told you they would be."

"I'm a mother. I can't *not* worry."

Derek glanced over at the door. No customers at the moment. "Tell me about your son."

He knew immediately he'd said the exact right thing. Gaby's face lit up with a brilliant smile. "Sandy. He's five. He's beautiful and smart and learns so fast. Here, I'll show you a picture."

She turned her phone toward him. The child who beamed at Derek from the photo was clearly related to Gaby; he had her dimples and pointy chin, though his curls were lighter, a medium brown to Gaby's black.

"He's my whole world," Gaby said softly. "His father was a cad and he's long gone, good riddance to bad rubbish, but I have no regrets because I got Sandy. I can't imagine anything happening to him. I couldn't take it."

"Nothing will happen." Derek wanted to smooth her raven hair away from her face. He settled for reaching out to place a comforting hand on her arm.

And he knew in that instant that his bear's protective instincts had expanded to include not just his mate but her family as well. Just as he'd rather die than see anything happen to Gaby, he also couldn't let anything happen to her son or her mother.

They were hers, which meant they were now his as well.

GABY

Derek's hand was warm and strong on her arm. As she looked up at him, it was all she could do not to throw herself into his arms.

Being a single mom meant having to be a pillar of strength. She had her mother to help her, but with Mama recovering from hip surgery, Gaby had to be there for her mother as well as her son.

She hadn't realized how much she'd needed someone to be there for *her*.

And for all the things she kept telling herself about why this was a bad idea—Derek was a professional bodyguard; he was protecting her because it was his *job*—she felt as if she'd been swept away into something too big to stop.

Sandy would have been the one big sticking point. She couldn't be with a man who couldn't accept her son. But now Derek knew about Sandy and he didn't seem to mind ... unlike every other guy she'd dated since Sandy had been born.

It just *felt* different with Derek. When she'd first laid eyes on him, it was like something that had been missing all her life had clicked into place. She'd never felt anything like it before.

And the way he was looking at her with that warmth in his eyes ...

It was like there was a magnetic attraction drawing the two of them together. Gaby started to lean forward—

And Polly came out of the back, dusting off her hands on her apron. Gaby jerked away, trying to recover her poise and look professional.

Polly glanced between the two of them. Her gaze softened and became almost maternal. "Gaby. Go home."

"What?" Gaby protested. She could feel herself flushing. "I thought you were okay with the whole thing—uh, Derek staying here to guard me, I mean—"

"I'm fine with it, but I don't see any reason for you to work a shift and a half today after the shock you had this morning." Polly patted her on the shoulder. "I really appreciate you staying through the breakfast rush, hon. But I've called Mei and she can come in and do the closing shift."

"It really is okay. I just got off the phone with Mama—"

"Gaby. Gabriella. Dear." Polly leaned in and murmured in her ear, "Let the nice tall bodyguard take you somewhere safe. We'll be fine here."

Gaby sighed and gave up on fighting it. She hugged Polly. "Thanks. I'll be here for the opening shift tomorrow, I promise."

"I'll expect you, but give me a call right away if you can't make it, okay?"

Gaby nodded. "Thanks for looking out for me."

At the door of the coffee shop, Derek stopped her. "I'm going to take a quick look to make sure the street's clear. Stay behind me, but touch my back lightly so I know exactly where you are, especially if I have to draw my gun. That's going to be our procedure when we enter a new location from now on. Okay?"

She nodded, moving a little closer so she could rest her hand tentatively against his back. She hadn't expected it to feel so intimate. She could feel his muscles flexing as he moved, one hand hovering near his gun. He seemed so sure and capable. She'd never felt safer.

"Clear," Derek said quietly.

Gaby took her hand away from his back, with an instant's regret as her fingers left the warmth of his shirt-clad skin, and followed him outside. As she left the coffee shop, she glanced back to see Polly looking after them with an expression that could only be described as knowing.

Then she was out on the street, which looked perfectly normal, bustling with pedestrians and vehicles as it always did at this time of day. The armored car was gone now, and the patch of sidewalk in front of the credit union looked no different from any other part of the sidewalk. Gaby doubted if the people going in and out of its swinging glass door knew that a robbery had taken place this morning right where they were walking.

If she hadn't seen it happen herself, she would've been one of those oblivious pedestrians herself. Now she wondered how many other life-changing events she'd walked past, never knowing.

"How are you holding up?" Derek asked, placing a hand in the middle of her back. His fingers were warm and strong, and more bracing than her half-finished latte.

"I don't know," she admitted. "It feels like ... like the cover has been ripped off the world. Does that make any sense? Everything's different. But everyone's going on like it's just the same."

"That's perfectly normal when you've witnessed an act of

violence," Derek told her. "The department can probably hook you up with a counselor if you need one."

Yeah, and how was she supposed to pay for *that*? Gaby shook her head. "I'm doing okay, I think. All I need is—"

You, she wanted to say. But that was ridiculous. She'd only just met him.

And yet there was that coming-home feeling, as if the only place she ever wanted to be was right here by his side.

As she started walking down the street toward her usual transit stop, Derek stopped her with a hand. "What's wrong?" she asked.

"Where are you going?"

"My bus stop," Gaby said. Her feet had automatically turned in that direction; she hadn't even thought about it.

"Oh no, no." Derek shook his head. "You're not using public transportation, not 'til this is cleared up. I'll drive you."

With a possible shape-changing killer after her, she wasn't about to argue, especially if it meant not hassling with the bus. Her eyes widened slightly when Derek escorted her to his car, a classic black Mustang parked outside the coffee shop.

"So you're a car guy," she said, running a thumb across the leather seat before sitting down.

"I like an engine with some muscle."

"Get in a lot of car chases, do you?" Her heart fluttered as the car doors closed, shutting out the city. It felt suddenly, startlingly intimate, just the two of them in the Mustang's front seats.

"I believe in being prepared. Go ahead and lock your door."

She popped the lock down; he'd already locked his. "This feels so weird. Like I'm being completely paranoid."

"Better to take precautions than to be caught off guard if something does happen." He turned to her, his brown eyes very serious. "But I'm not letting anything happen you on my watch, Gaby."

"I believe you," she whispered. She could feel the conviction of his words.

And finally, after all the interruptions, it seemed like the most natural thing in the world to lean forward and meet his lips with hers.

It felt like a circuit closing, as if the attraction between them could only be resisted for a little while, never stopped. Derek kissed back with fervor, his mouth opening under hers to claim the sweetness of her kiss. He brought his hands up to bury his fingers in her hair, and she succumbed to the temptation to touch the flat, hard planes of his stomach, her hand sliding to rest on his waist.

When their lips parted, she gazed at him in a daze. She'd never been kissed like that before. Her heart was fluttering madly now, her chest full of heat, and tension grew between her legs, aching for the only kind of release that could relieve it.

"Wow," Derek breathed.

Gaby had to swallow a couple of times to get her voice back. "I shouldn't have—"

"Yeah, you should have," Derek said softly, and with one strong hand he brought her in for another kiss. This one was gentler and longer, and the sensation went straight down through her body to her aching sex.

She *wanted* him; oh, she wanted him. Her body ached for him. These touches didn't salve her need; they only made it grow.

Derek let go with a few little nibbles at her lips. "Where do you want to go?" he asked, swiping a thumb over the corner of her mouth. "I could take you straight home. Or we could go inspect the hotel room that's apparently been secured to keep you safe."

A hotel room ... with no mother, no small child. A bed with clean sheets that she didn't have to wash. And, most importantly, privacy.

"Hotel," she declared.

"I was hoping you'd say that." Derek was grinning as he put the car in gear.

He took a circuitous route to the hotel. Gaby had lived in this city all her life, and she still wasn't sure where they were going until they pulled into an underground parking garage.

"Didn't want to take a chance on being followed," Derek explained.

"I'm totally fine with that." She got out her phone, guiltily trying to figure out how to text her mom and explain that she was taking off work early, that she was fine but she wasn't going home yet because she was with her incredibly hot bodyguard ...

There was absolutely no way she could explain this to her mom in a series of texts. Not without immediately getting a phone call and a torrent of the Spanglish that Luisa Diaz lapsed into when she was upset.

Mama and Sandy are perfectly safe, she told herself. *A cop is with them. And I'm safe with Derek.*

All her life, she'd been cautious and careful. She'd always done the safe, sensible, responsible thing. She had put other people before herself, every single time.

Maybe it was time to do something a little bit foolish and crazy. Something just for her.

"Remember the procedure from earlier," Derek told her as they got out of the car. "I'm going to clear the stairwell and lobby before you enter, okay?"

"Okay," she said quietly, subdued at the reminder that they weren't here for fun. (Not *just* for fun, anyway, said a tiny little voice inside her—the long-suppressed wild'n'crazy Gabriella who had been squashed down beneath serious, sensible Gaby.) There was a very serious reason why she'd gotten off early from work.

But she *did* feel safe with Derek. It wasn't just having a big, muscular guy at her side. It was a bone-deep conviction that he would do whatever it took to protect her. And she thought that getting away from the coffee shop, where everything had happened, was helping too.

Derek left her sitting in a cluster of chairs in the hotel lobby while he went to check in. It wasn't a fantastically high-class hotel, just a big chain hotel of the conference center type, but it was still miles beyond anything she'd ever been able to afford for herself on a barista's salary. On the rare occasions when she and her family went anywhere, it was strictly Motel 6 all the way.

I bet they have room service here, she thought, looking up at the high ceiling of the lobby, brushed by the leaves of potted ornamental trees. *I wonder if they'll let me bring Mama and Sandy here too. They'd be safer here, wouldn't they? My mom would absolutely love it. I hope they have a big tub, maybe a Jacuzzi ...*

Derek came back and handed her a key card. "Room 419. For the record, we're checked in as Quincy and Mary Jones."

"Er, Quincy?"

"Blame Keegan for that one," Derek said with a grimace. He shepherded her into the elevator, not in a pushy way, but she couldn't help noticing how he interposed himself between her and the lobby until the doors closed. And then it was just the two of them in the elevator.

And very soon, just the two of them in a hotel room.

Gaby cleared her throat, trying to distract herself from his presence—so large, so near. She wondered if he knew what his defensive body language was doing to her. *Mess with this woman and die,* his stance said. Of course, he was a bodyguard. It was his *job*. But there was something about having all of that attention focused on her that was *doing things* to her, especially when it was coming from someone as completely ripped and good looking as Derek ...

"So what's the long-term plan here?" she asked, to stop herself from climbing him right here in the elevator. "I've got a busy life, a full-time job and night classes, not to mention my family."

"Well, since you've made it very clear that you won't be putting any part of that life on hold just because of the small matter of your life possibly being in danger ..." He said it without rancor, instead wearing a small grin that looked almost admiring. "Then I guess I'll be coming with you for all of those things."

"What, going to class with me?"

"I can wait in the hall."

"Derek—no! You can't stay with me 24-7. You must have a life of your own to get back to."

"This is my job," he pointed out. "You're my life now."

Before she could tease out the tangled meanings behind *that*, the doors opened on their floor. Derek touched her arm, positioning her subtly behind him as he stepped out into the hallway. The elevator door started to close. Gaby touched it to keep it open until Derek looked back and nodded.

"Is it always going to be like ... this, though?" she asked as they went down the hall in close proximity to each other, his arm almost but not quite brushing hers. "I mean, you'll need to sleep and eat and ... and you must have friends, family— you can't put everything on hold for me."

"Only until the cops catch the guy," Derek said. He swiped the key card in the door and poked his head into the room, taking a quick look around before letting her in.

Right. This was only temporary. She tried to convince herself that she wasn't disappointed—not at the idea of getting back to her regular life, but having Derek out of it. To distract herself from the clutch of unhappiness in her chest, she looked around.

After the nice lobby, the hotel room was less palatial than she'd hoped, although there was room for two beds, a desk and chair, and a minifridge. It was much bigger than her bedroom at home. Gaby whipped out her phone.

"Now what are you doing?" Derek asked, coming out of the bathroom. She hadn't heard him do anything in there; she was pretty sure he was just checking it in case of assassins lurking behind the shower curtain. He slung his jacket over the back of the room's only chair.

"I'm taking pictures to show Mama and Sandy. I guess this must be an everyday kind of thing for you, but I've never stayed in a hotel this nice." She started to hold up the phone toward him, then lowered it. "Is it violating your bodyguard rules or anything to take a picture of you? I mean, would that like, blow your cover?"

"Bodyguards aren't like undercover cops. The whole point is that we're *supposed* to be seen."

"Well, in that case, say cheese!"

He smiled dutifully, and when she put the phone away, she was surprised to see how soft his expression was—almost wistful. "Your family is lucky to have you, Gaby. Every time you talk about them, I can see how much they mean to you."

"I hope they'll be safe," she said quietly, setting her purse on the desk. This kept feeling like a fun adventure ... until it didn't anymore.

Derek touched her arm gently, and when she didn't pull away, he put an arm around her and guided her away from the desk. He sat on the foot of the nearest bed and drew her down beside him.

"Gaby, I haven't known you very long, but I can already tell you're one of the strongest, most determined people I've ever met." Derek touched her chin, turning her face up towards his. "They're going to be fine. *You're* going to be fine."

"I like it when you tell me that," she whispered, lips parting. "Say it again."

"You're really fine, Gaby," he whispered back, his lips inches from hers, and the corners of her mouth pulled back in a grin.

"You too," she murmured before his mouth closed on hers and rational thought fled.

He kissed with the same passionate intensity that he did everything else. Derek Ruger wasn't a man who lived life halfway, she could tell already, and after spending her whole life being safe, being sensible, she could feel those chains of caution loosening and falling away under his touch. She had never been kissed like this before. If she hadn't been sitting down already, her knees would have folded.

She surfaced from the kiss to find that his hand had worked its way under the bottom edge of her T-shirt. Both *her* hands were spread across the smooth muscle of his stomach, and before she could stop herself, she dipped her fingers under the waistband of his jeans. She could just touch the top of his underwear. *Boxers or briefs?* She had a feeling she was about to find out.

"Don't stop," she gasped, and recaptured his mouth with hers.

They kissed madly as they fumbled with each other's clothing. He unclasped her bra under her shirt; she gasped against his mouth as her breasts swung free. She was already wet as she climbed into his lap, legs spread so she could grind herself against him. Through his tight jeans she felt the massive stiffness of his erection.

They had to break the kiss to strip off their T-shirts. She straddled his lap as she pulled it over her head, and when her face emerged from the gray fabric, she found that he'd done the same in a single fast motion. Now she got an up-close look at that amazing, chiseled body she'd seen earlier. It was all working muscle, not the bulging body of a bulked-up gym rat.

She just wanted to touch him all over, *feel* him all over, bury her face in him.

Her whole life had been about self-control. It was about denying herself that candy bar so she could save the dollar to pay bus fare. It was about working her way through classes no matter how boring the subject matter, so she could get her business degree and earn a better living for her family. It was about working second shifts at the coffee shop so she could buy toys for her son's birthday and pay the copay on her mom's pain meds.

The only reckless thing she'd ever done in her whole life was her fling with her son's father, and she couldn't regret it because Sandy was the best thing that had ever happened to her. But she'd come out of that affair with the firm conviction that it was the last reckless thing she'd ever do in her life.

She had been wrong. So wrong.

It wasn't about keeping control all the time. It was about losing control with the right person.

She was losing control and it felt *so good*.

With her bra dangling from one arm by its strap, she pushed Derek down on the bed so she could straddle his hips properly. Making a husky groan deep in his throat, he let her, even though he was strong enough to fling her off without breaking a sweat.

He smelled wonderful. No hint of cologne or hair product, just a faint whiff of shaving foam and soap to accent the musky, spicy smell of male skin. She kissed his collarbones, his powerfully muscled shoulders, and ran her hands across the rough, ridged skin of the scars on his stomach and side.

On anyone else, those scars might have marred the perfection of his skin, but on Derek they did nothing except enhance the whole package. He was a dangerous man who made a living by fighting. She'd never been with anyone like that before.

And yet he was incredibly gentle as he stroked her skin, caressing her breasts, running a big thumb over her nipples. His eyes, when she pulled back to look into his face, were soft with a kind of warm wonder, like he was drinking in the sight of her.

At any other time she'd have soaked up that worshipful gaze like a flower seeking the sun, but right now all she wanted him to do was wrestle her down and fill her with the erect cock pressing through his jeans against her inner thigh. She undid her jeans and rose up to her knees to push them down over her hips, followed by her panties. Derek obviously got the picture; he was fumbling with the snap of his jeans already.

He was a briefs man, she discovered as his jeans went the way of her own.

And he was also huge. She'd never been with anyone that big. Right now, though, she had no concerns about whether he'd fit. She was soaking wet and about as ready as she'd ever been. At the sight of him, any last vestiges of control fled.

"Derek, I need you—now—"

Responding to her cry, he pushed into her, and she threw her head back in pure pleasure, digging her fingers into his chest. Each stroke pressed gloriously against her slippery inner walls, sliding in and out as she thrust back vigorously.

Derek rolled her over on the bed so he could get his mouth on hers, kissing her with a clashing of teeth as he thrust into her. Their bodies were tangled together, sweat-damp and burning with shared need. She could feel herself mounting toward orgasm and she didn't hold back. She was aware of his body shaking with the effort to control himself, to keep from reaching his own climax before she was ready.

She went over the edge with a powerful shock, her mind going numb in the throes of the best orgasm she'd ever had. Derek shuddered through his own shocks as he held her, and finally they collapsed on the bed, coming down from the high together.

DEREK

Sated and exhausted, all Derek wanted to do was lie beside his mate all afternoon.

But he couldn't. There were plans to make. Check-ins to perform.

His mate was in danger and he wasn't about to be less than fully vigilant.

Gaby made a tiny protesting noise as he pulled away from her and sat up. He swung his legs off the edge of the bed, and untangled his wadded-up jeans to get his phone out of the pocket.

"What are you doing?" Gaby asked, propping herself up on one elbow.

She looked amazing like this, her thick black hair hanging in a sex-tousled mass over her light brown shoulder. Derek smiled to allay the anxiety in her eyes. "Just checking with Keegan to see how the investigation's going. No point in worrying unduly if they've already caught the guy."

He sent off a quick text to Keegan, and another to the owner of the bar where he worked as a part-time bouncer to let them know that he wouldn't be coming in on his usual night this week.

Gaby sat up and stretched, raising her breasts gloriously before her arms dropped back down. "So what's it like, being a bodyguard? Lifestyles of the rich and famous? Do you jet-set around the world, guarding famous people?"

Derek couldn't help laughing. "Not exactly. More like babysitting the petty and drunk. I don't do much of this kind of work anymore, and when I do, it's mainly event security, short-term gigs as supplemental security for out-of-town celebrities' or politicians' families, and that kind of thing. Distinctly unglamorous. It's mostly a matter of escorting drunk college kids out of nightclubs."

"You don't normally work with the police?"

"Only when Keegan asks me to," Derek said. "He's an old friend. We go back a ways."

"School buddies?" she asked.

"Something like that." The last thing he wanted to do was tell her about the darker part of his past, which was inextricably tangled up with meeting Keegan in South America. Tales of gun battles had no place in this quiet hotel room; he had no business telling those stories to this soft, trusting woman with her gentle brown eyes and gentler hands.

There was a wildcat side to her, though. As he reached for his T-shirt, he looked down with a grin at the scratches on his chest.

Which made Gaby notice it, too. She gasped in dismay. "Oh, my gosh. Did I do that?"

"Sure did." He traced one of the faint pink lines with his fingertip, and then raised the finger to touch her lips. "Hey, if I wanted you to stop, I'd have said."

"I guess I got a little carried away."

"No, you got exactly the right amount of carried away,"

Derek corrected her. With a grin, he leaned over to kiss her. She hesitated before settling into the kiss.

His mate. Warm and pliant and lovely, with the smell of sex on her skin.

He would do anything to keep her safe. Even from his own past.

~

They ordered a late lunch from room service, which Gaby was adorably delighted with, even though all she ordered was a burger and fries.

"Look, I'm used to staying in the sort of hotel where you pass your credit card to the clerk through a security grille," Gaby said defensively. "I feel like I'm in a movie."

If this was a movie, hopefully it was a meet-cute chick flick and not the sort of movie Derek's life tended to resemble, which were more of the helicopters-and-explosions, Schwarzenegger and Van Damme type. Derek decided to keep his doubts to himself.

Gaby dipped a french fry in her ketchup. "Are we going to bring Mama and Sandy here?"

"It would be easier if you were all in the same place," Derek said. He felt his bear stir beneath his skin, itching to be able to protect his mate's family personally. "However, if the Ghost does come after you, it might be better if you *weren't* together. They're safe enough where they are, for now."

Gaby's mouth rounded in an "O" of shock. "I didn't even *think* ... just being with them might put them in danger, wouldn't it? I don't want to do that!"

This was all so new to her, and Derek pushed down a surge of fury at the Ghost for knocking away the foundations of her safe, secure world, forcing her into the hunters-and-prey mode of thinking for the first time in her life. The whole reason why people like him existed was so that people like her didn't have to think about those things.

But she seemed to be holding up well so far.

"You can see your family this evening, but we should probably spend the night at the hotel, just to be safe."

Gaby nodded and scooted a little closer to him. "So tell me about this guy who's after me. What did you call him? Ghost? What *is* he? I know he's, uh ... a guy who turns into a bear. Was he bitten by a radioactive bear, or what?"

"No, shifters are born that way." Derek hesitated briefly. "*I* was born that way."

Gaby gave a little nod. He still couldn't tell if she believed him about turning into a bear. She'd seen the Ghost do it, but that was one thing. The Ghost was a scary apparition, the bad guy who had chased her and tried to kill her. Knowing the guy she'd been talking to, the guy she'd just had sex with, spent part of his life as a grizzly bear was a lot to take in.

"The Ghost is muscle for hire. I don't even know his real name. When I fought with him—when he gave me these ..." He touched the scars through the fabric of his T-shirt. "He was working for a drug cartel. I assume he's doing something like that here, too, working for a local mobster or drug dealer."

"So, if the cops can find his boss, they can find him too, right? And stop him?"

"Yep," Derek said, although he was thinking that if the police closed in on the Ghost, he'd probably disappear just like his namesake. He had a habit of doing that, vanishing from one part of the world only to pop up somewhere else, months or years later.

His phone vibrated and he reached for it. There was a new text. "Hey, speak of the devil. Keegan says they haven't found the Ghost yet, but sources say he's working as mob muscle for a local crime family. They're running down those leads right now." He gave her a quick smile. "You might be back to your old life before you know it."

For some reason, this made her look slightly downcast before she smiled back. "That's good news."

Before Derek could probe the mystery of why she didn't look delighted, another text came in. "Also, Keegan says your family's security detail is about to change shifts. He wants to know if I can take it for a few hours this evening; then he can put another team of his guys on it for the night shift."

Now she did brighten. "Oh yes, let's do that! I can't wait 'til you meet my mom and Sandy."

... *shit*. He hoped his dismay didn't show, let alone his panic.

He was going to have to meet his mate's family.

The family she was completely devoted to.

Including a mother who was probably going to be less than thrilled when her daughter showed up with a big, scarred bruiser in tow.

A shifter family would understand, of course. Your mate wasn't someone you chose; the mate bond chose you. It was like a lightning strike. Your mate *couldn't* be unsuitable, no matter their outward appearance. Your souls knew each other at first sight.

But humans did things differently.

"Derek?" Gaby asked, hesitating.

"Yeah, that'll be great," he said, to himself as much as to her. "I'll just text Keegan and let him know."

Gaby gave Derek directions to her apartment building. He pulled up behind the unmarked police car, which he recognized by guesswork: it was the only car, in the long row of street-parked vehicles, with anyone in it, a man and a woman who had their heads bent together in a sort of halfhearted necking posture.

Derek knocked on the window and the two of them broke apart. When the window rolled halfway down, he recognized the woman inside. He'd met her at the police barbecues that Keegan had a habit of inviting him to.

She recognized him, too. "You're the lieutenant's body-guard buddy, right? I guess this means we stand relieved, JJ," she said to her partner.

"Thank God," the man beside her said with fervor. "If I have to pretend to kiss you one more time, my wife's gonna kill me when I get home."

The female cop rolled her eyes. "Like it's such a treat getting *your* beard burn on *my* face."

"No sign of anything hinky, right?" Derek asked.

"Nah, just the usual pedestrian traffic. We saw the old

lady and the little boy leave the building awhile back, then come back with some shopping bags."

"I hope she was using her walker," Gaby said anxiously, pushing up next to Derek. "Mama hates using the walker in public, but she's not supposed to walk all the way to the store without it, let alone try to carry anything."

The female cop glanced at her partner, who shrugged and said, "She was pushing some kind of little cart-type thing."

"Yes, that's her walker. It's got a basket on it, for putting things in," Gaby explained to Derek.

The security situation got worse and worse. An infirm, elderly lady and a little kid ... and just thinking about it, he could feel his bear flexing its claws and showing its teeth, ready to defend his mate's family.

"Anyway, we're headed back to the station." The female cop raised a hand and their car pulled away from the curb.

"Oh, I forgot to ask them if Mama was actually using the walker or just wheeling it along," Gaby fretted. "She does that too. She had hip surgery just recently, and she's supposed to be taking it easy, but with me working all day, she has to do most of the shopping—"

"Gaby, your mom's fine." He squeezed her hand and forced his nervousness off his face. "Come on, let's go meet them. Which floor are you on?"

"The third." She unlocked the door and let him in. "At least it's a secure building."

"Just the one entrance?"

"There's a utility door in the back."

"Do people use it?"

"None of the residents have keys, but the door opens from the inside, so sometimes people go out that way as a shortcut through the alley."

Which meant the Ghost could get in that way. He wouldn't even have to wait for someone to leave, come to think of it. With his powerful polar bear body, he could probably force either door; they were designed to stand up to human burglars, not a half ton of apex predator.

And *that* meant having a guard on the front of the building wasn't going to be enough, especially under the cover of darkness. The Ghost could come and go from the back at will. Moving Gaby's family to the hotel was probably the best option.

"Is something wrong?" Gaby asked anxiously, moving closer to him.

"No, just thinking about security details. It's my job; I can't help it." As his mate, she was already picking up on his emotional state more easily. It wasn't precisely telepathy so much as a strong sense of being in tune with each other; they were more aware of the subtle tells of each other's faces and bodies and, in his case, scents. And at least some of the nervousness she sensed in him was because of meeting her family, so he tried to crush it down so as not to alarm her unduly.

"Third floor, right?" he said, and she nodded.

She let him check the stairwell before they stepped inside. By now it was becoming second nature for both of them; she automatically fell back as they approached a door, stepping behind him without needing to be told and resting her hand against his back, the softest of touches as if a butterfly had alighted there.

He'd known her for half a day and already he could work more smoothly with her than with teammates he'd worked with for months in the past.

But that was what having a mate meant. She was a true partner, joined to him body and soul.

On the third floor, she took the lead, stopping in front of a scarred wooden door. Derek made a move to stop her as she got out her keys, but aborted in mid-movement, realizing he could hear the happy babble of a playing child from behind the door, with occasional interjections from a woman's voice. If anything had happened in their absence, and in particular, if the Ghost was waiting for them inside, he didn't think a small child could be induced to sound that naturally happy.

Gaby unlocked the door.

"Mama!" came a joyful squeal, and a little boy with a riot of brown curls bounded up off the floor, where he'd been sitting surrounded by blocks and snap-together toys, and flung himself at her knees. "You're home early!"

"Oof! Watch out! Don't kneecap me!" She swept him up in her arms. "How was your day? Did you and Grandma Luisa have a nice time?"

"We went to the park! I petted a dog that was very soft and I asked the lady before I petted him and she said I could. She said his name was Tiger. I'm going to name my dog Tiger when I have a dog. When can I have a dog?"

"When we live in a place that allows pets," Gaby said in a tone which suggested this was a question she'd answered a number of times already.

She stepped forward into the apartment, with a giggling Sandy dangling from her neck. Derek followed her and closed the door quietly behind them.

The apartment smelled of potpourri and warm, pleasant cooking smells. It was small but tidy. The furniture crowded the living room somewhat, but had been arranged so there was room to move about between couch and armchair, coffee table and TV stand. The walls held an assortment of collectible plates with cute big-eyed children and animals on them, framed paintings of flowers, and a large gilt crucifix on the wall opposite the TV, above a bookcase crowded with paperbacks.

Derek had felt out of place in the coffee shop, but in this

warm, homey room, he felt a thousand times more so. This was exactly the kind of place that men like him didn't belong, not with the air of darkness and danger that surrounded him. He shouldn't have come—

"Gabriella?" An older woman appeared from the nooklike kitchen, coming out from behind a freestanding cabinet that held the family's dishes. She was limping slightly and drying her hands on a dish towel, which she threw over her shoulder before flinging her arms around Gaby, child and all. "What a terrible day for you, my heart! And you didn't answer my texts!"

"Mama, I texted you from the car to let you know I was bringing someone for dinner."

"Yes, but you didn't answer the next three texts asking *who*. Oh!" Gabriella's mother switched her attention to Derek, like lightning. Startled, he found his right hand engulfed in both of her small, strong ones. "Is it this fine young man? When I said you should find a nice man, I didn't know you would take my advice so quickly!"

"Mama! This is the man I told you about who is keeping me safe. He is my bodyguard. Derek," Gaby sighed, "this is my mother, Luisa Diaz, and my son Sandy."

Some parents resemble their children closely. This wasn't the case with Luisa and Gaby—Gaby was curvy and medium height with a cascade of thick black hair; Luisa was short and round all over, her face made even rounder by its frame of brown curls.

But he could still see echoes of Luisa in her mother, especially around Luisa's generous mouth, in her eyes, in the set of her stubborn chin. He thought he could see where Gaby had gotten her courage and determination from.

He tried to let go of his feelings of discomfort. If Luisa felt that he was a man who shouldn't be around her daughter, he had no doubt that she would have told him so. Instead, she was beaming up at him.

"Ma'am, it's a pleasure to meet you," he said, closing his left hand around the short fingers clasping his right. "Your daughter's safety is my only priority."

Luisa turned to Gaby with a wide smile. "I like him! You can keep him," she declared.

"Gosh, thanks, Mama." Gaby rolled her eyes and smiled at Derek, but despite the mock exasperation, she looked genuinely relieved. And he felt as if he'd passed a test.

"I'm going to want to hear the entire story, every bit of it, but not in front of small pitchers with big ears." Luisa tweaked Sandy's ear, making him squirm. "But first, we should eat."

"Can I help with anything?" Derek asked. In retrospect he should probably have thought to stop somewhere and pick up something to bring along for the meal. He hadn't even thought about it. He was completely unused to deal with family occasions.

"No, no. You're a guest." Luisa hustled him to the couch. "Gaby, set the table while I check the casserole. Alejo," she added to the little boy, "come here and help me check if the oven timer has failed to ring again."

Derek helped Gaby drag out the table, which turned out to be folded in a corner, since there wasn't room in the small apartment to set it up without pushing the furniture out of the way. Gaby shook a flowered tablecloth over it and got down dishes from the cabinet. As she passed them to Derek to lay on the table, he noticed that they were nice dishes, with little roses on them; they made him think of a set his grandmother used to have.

"Are these antiques?" he asked.

"Only in the sense that my mother is an antique."

"I heard that!" came a call from the kitchen.

"I'm sorry, Mama!" Gaby said, winking at Derek. "No, Mama and Papa bought these when they were married." She knelt to open a drawer in the bottom of the cabinet, and got out several rolled cloth napkins.

"I promised on my wedding day to Alejandro—God rest his soul—that I would always set a nice table," Luisa declared from the kitchen. "And I always shall. Gaby, put the flowers from the top of the bookcase on the table. The vase with the sunflowers. It will make a nice centerpiece."

Gaby handed the napkins to Derek and went to get the vase off the bookcase. "Before she got sick, my mother was the office manager at a rental car franchise," she told Derek softly, wearing a trace of a smile as she set the vase in the center of the tablecloth. "Now she's got no one to manage except her daughter and grandson."

"She's not badly sick, I hope?" Derek asked, just as quietly, glancing into the kitchen where Sandy was standing on a stepstool and helping Luisa rinse a serving spoon in the sink.

"She's much better now than she was," Gaby murmured back. "She's always had problems with arthritis in her hips, but it got so bad she couldn't even sit up, let alone work. She had to have both hips replaced, and she's just recovering from the second surgery."

His poor, brave mate. No wonder she was so serious and responsible. She had been carrying the weight of her family's worries on her shoulders, all alone. Derek brushed a hand down her elbow, eliciting a brief, pleased shiver. *You don't have to carry it alone anymore,* he wanted to say with that gesture of support.

"I see you are telling all our family secrets," Luisa said, coming out of the kitchen with a casserole dish in both hands. Sandy trailed her, clutching an iron trivet. "Now put that there, sweet one, beside the flowers." Sandy stretched to set the trivet very carefully with both hands, and Luisa put the casserole dish on it.

"Mama, you aren't supposed to be carrying heavy things," Gaby fretted.

"It's not so heavy compared to this one." Luisa tousled Sandy's curls. "I pick him up a dozen times a day."

"Yes, you're not supposed to be doing that either. Derek, what would you like to drink? We have, uh, apple juice and milk, I'm afraid."

Her slightly abashed expression made him smile. "Milk is fine. It's good for healthy bones. Right, Sandy?" he asked the little boy who had climbed into the chair next to him, staring at him with open curiosity. "Or, did your grandmother call you Alejo?"

"Alejandro," the little boy said. "I'm named after Abuelo Alejo who is dead. Who are you named after?"

"No one. I'm just named Derek."

"That's a crane," the boy said promptly.

"... what?"

"He means 'derrick,'" Gaby said, setting a glass of milk in front of each of them. "Except it's not exactly like a crane, kiddo. What's the difference?"

Sandy screwed his face up. "A crane is tall and—no—"

"A crane is a bird," Luisa said with a mischievous smile, reaching over to unroll Sandy's napkin for him.

"Oh, Mama, don't confuse him! There's a new building going up on the next street over," Gaby told Derek, "and we're learning about all the construction equipment. Sandy is fascinated by big machines right now."

"I remember going through a big-trucks phase too," Derek said to Sandy, but absently, because something had caught his attention. He couldn't quite put his finger on it, but his bear, which had been quiescent inside him, had begun to stir. Something was bothering it.

63

"I prefer the trucks; it is better than Gaby's horse phase," Luisa said.

"Mama!"

"What? At least Alejo doesn't ask me constantly if he can have a real bulldozer, not like you asking for a pony six times a day. Where would we have put it, in the kitchen?"

"I was perfectly aware we couldn't have a pony in an apartment in the city even at Sandy's age, Mama—oh, Derek, where are you going?" she asked as he rose from the table, reaching a hand after him. "I'm sorry, this is just our family's usual sort of dinnertime conversation. Don't let us scare you off!"

"I'm the one who should apologize. Excuse me," Derek said, as politely as he could with his bear increasingly tense in his chest. "Is there an opening window in the kitchen?"

Luisa started to rise, but Gaby hopped up. "Mama, you shouldn't be getting up and down. I'll show you, Derek. There's actually a very small balcony, really more like a fire escape except without the escape part. You aren't feeling unwell, are you?" she asked anxiously, hovering close by his side.

"No, I'm fine. It's not that."

Gaby let them out onto a tiny balcony—she hadn't been joking; it was just wide enough to accommodate a cheap plastic chair (with a cushion on the seat and a book lying on it) and a large pot with a healthy-looking tomato plant in it. More plants, giving off pleasant herbal smells, were lined up on the railing.

"Did you hear something?" Gaby murmured.

"I'm not sure." He was glad his mate was here, close enough to touch, since his bear was getting increasingly agitated. Having her hip pressed against him and the smell of her skin (still lightly spiced with sex, even though she'd showered at the hotel) was distracting. But having her back in the living room would have been even more distracting, where she was out of sight.

Something subconscious had set off his bear's finally honed danger sense. He wished he could figure out what was bothering it. He trusted those instincts. The problem was, in the complicated modern world, his bear's idea of what constituted danger wasn't always accurate. Right now it could be anything from a distant car alarm to a smell that had triggered some buried memory of another time he'd been attacked. It was so much easier in the mountains, where his bear's instincts were adapted to the world around it, a world without cars or high-rise buildings.

If the Ghost is here, he's not being obvious about it. I don't hear him, or smell him ...

"Derek, how worried should I be?" Gaby's eyes were wide, staring up at his.

Trusting him. Trusting him to protect her.

He wanted to tell her not to worry, but *he* was worried. Something was upsetting his bear. And it wasn't anything obvious, which made him even more worried.

"Well, if we're not in danger, we should go back inside," Gaby whispered. "We're being awfully rude, hiding out here with dinner cooling on the table. My mom might get the wrong idea."

"That would be terrible," he murmured, sliding a hand down to cup her round bottom, even while his sharp shifter senses tried to sieve through all the many smells and sounds of the city, trying to find the one thing that had tripped his bear's danger instinct.

The anxiety pinching Gaby's face was chased away by a smile, as he'd hoped. "*You're* terrible," she said, swatting at his hand with no real force.

He caught her fingers, caging them with his own, and

grinned at her. God, being around her was like nothing he'd ever experienced. She made him feel light. Playful.

"I'll show you how terrible I can be. Later."

Gaby wrinkled her nose, looking amused. "You really need to work on your sweet talk, buddy."

He opened his mouth to respond, when he finally caught a whiff of something that struck a wrong note in the sounds and smells of an ordinary, peaceful city evening.

Smoke.

He hadn't noticed it before, with the cooking smells to cover it up. But now that the wind had changed, there was no mistaking it.

Gaby instantly sensed the tension in him. "What is it?"

Before he could answer, the building's fire alarm went off.

"Oh no," Gaby gasped, and darted into the kitchen. "Mother!"

"I hear it," Derek heard her mother say calmly. "Come on, Alejo. Dinner will have to wait."

Derek leaned over the railing. He couldn't see any smoke, but he could smell it more strongly now.

Ghost. It has to be. It could be a coincidence—but he was betting it wasn't. He'd thought Ghost would wait until nightfall to strike. But what better opportunity could there be? Ghost had seen the cops leave; he'd seen Derek go into the building with Gaby. *And regardless of whether he's after me or her, now he's got both.*

And dinnertime would be the perfect opportunity, because no one would be going anywhere. They'd be busy and caught off guard. All the Ghost had to do was get everyone out of the building and then pick off his targets.

The question was, where would he be? Waiting out front, where the crowd was going to congregate, or in back of the building?

Front. Probably. It depended on how wary he expected them to be.

Derek turned away, steeling himself, and checked the load in his gun.

Inside, he found Luisa helping Sandy put his shoes on, while Gaby was grabbing items and shoving them into a backpack. "Sandy's birth certificate and vaccination records —Papa's photo album—what else do we need? We should have some clothes—" She yanked open a drawer and started stuffing items into the backpack.

Derek took her by the shoulders. "Gaby. It's not worth your life. We have to get you and your family out."

"Yes," she gasped. "Yes, of course." She stilled, looking up at him. "Derek, is it—Ghost?"

"We have to assume so," he said quietly. "It's not likely he'll try anything in a crowd." At least, it was better for her to think so. He didn't need panicking civilians on his hands. "Stay with me. We're going to be heading for the car and getting all of you out of here."

"Yes. That makes sense." She slung the backpack onto her back. "Mama, get your walker, would you?"

"I don't need to deal with that thing in a crowded stair-well, Gabriella—"

"You can't walk a block without it. Just get it, Mama, please? It folds up, so we'll carry it down the stairs."

They made a strange procession trooping out into the hallway. Luisa held Sandy's hand, while Gaby carried the folded-flat walker in one arm and had her other arm around her mother, the backpack dangling from her shoulder. The hallway was half full of panicked building residents, but Derek could no longer smell smoke. If *he* was in Ghost's place, trying to flush out his quarry, he wouldn't set the entire building on fire. That'd be a good way to end up in danger himself. He'd break into an empty apartment and create enough smoke to set off the building-wide fire alarms, which was the only thing he'd really need.

Still, they couldn't count on it, certainly not enough to stay inside a building that might be on fire. Around him, he saw old people, families, little kids. People were clutching bundles of belongings, or empty-handed and crying.

If the Ghost had done this, Derek thought grimly, he was going down.

As he shepherded his charges toward the stairwell, Derek realized that there were two entrances and exits downstairs, but a strategic bottleneck inside the building. Nobody would be using the elevator during a fire. So everyone had to go down the stairs.

I hope what I said to Gaby is right and he really won't attack in a crowd, because otherwise, we're all in trouble.

He paused at the stairwell door, causing a pile-up behind him, as he tried to figure out the best way to do this. Gaby was going to be the target, but the old woman and child were too vulnerable to leave unprotected. Danger would most likely come from below, but he couldn't see what was happening to Gaby and her family if he put them behind him. At times like this, working with a partner would really come in handy ...

"What's the holdup?" someone shouted angrily from behind.

"I'm going to have you three go in front," Derek told Gaby. "I'll be right behind you. Trust me."

"I do," she said softly, and with her arm around her mother, she nudged open the stairwell door with her elbow.

The four of them joined the crowd of fleeing residents jostling their way down the stairs. Derek took advantage of his natural size and generally intimidating nature to stay so close to Gaby that he was almost stepping on her heels. He could hear sirens wailing now. *Good. If we can just get out of the building, it ought to be easy to make our escape in the confusion, with emergency vehicles everywhere—*

At the bottom of the stairs, the Ghost was waiting in the hall.

It was a good location. Derek had to admire his strategic sense, if nothing else. Every person on the upper floors had to come out the door into the hallway. The stairwell door swung open and closed as each little family-sized knot of refugees pushed out into the hallway. As they reached the ground floor and Gaby started to push it open, Derek glimpsed sudden movement in the hall, going against the tide of escaping building residents.

"Move!" he snapped, pushing Gaby and her family unceremoniously out of the way.

Ghost slammed into him.

It was definitely Ghost. There was no mistaking those ice-pale eyes, not to mention the massive size of him. He was actually bigger than Derek, but Derek had fury on his side. Through sheer bodily force he pushed Ghost out into the hallway, slamming him into the wall so Gaby, her family, and the rest of the refugees could get out of the stairwell.

"Give it up, Ruger," Ghost snarled.

"Shut up!" Derek headbutted him, and as the Ghost reeled, Derek briefly freed a hand to hook his keys out of his pocket and fling them in Gaby's direction. "Gaby! Get to my car. Get out of here. I'll hold him off."

"What about you?" she protested.

"Just go!"

All he could do was hope Ghost still worked alone and didn't have a partner waiting out front. However, he suspected that if Ghost was working with someone, he wouldn't have risked an attack in the crowded hallway; he'd just have had both exits covered and made his move outside.

There was no choice but to gamble Gaby's life on it.

Ghost snarled and his canines lengthened as he went for Derek's neck. Derek twisted to take the bite on his shoulder rather than the throat, turning his body to knee Ghost in the stomach. Ghost tried to twist away to go after Gaby, but Derek kicked his legs out from under him and the two of them went down to the floor in a tangle.

They were too close together for Derek to try for his gun; he'd be just as likely to shoot himself. Ghost hadn't shifted completely, but his face lengthened into a muzzle as he snapped and bit at Derek, savaging his shoulder.

Derek's bear was fighting to get out, too, roaring its fury inside him. He struggled to hold it back. If they both erupted in a full-fledged shift, the building residents would have to deal with two battling, giant bears rolling around in the hallway.

Still, if Ghost shifted all the way, Derek wouldn't have a choice. He couldn't win in hand-to-claw combat against a polar bear.

Got to keep him from shifting—but how?

Talk to him.

When the human side was fully engaged, it made it harder to shift.

"What'd you do, set off a smoke bomb down here?"

"Grease fire," Ghost said indistinctly through his fangs.

"I'd admire your style if I didn't want to kill you for it. This is between you and me. Gaby has nothing to do with it." Too late he realized he'd used her nickname. He should have stuck to Ms. Diaz.

"She's a witness," Ghost growled. "She's nothing, all right —nothing but a job."

How dare he talk that way about our mate!

Derek roared in Ghost's face. He could feel his fingers trying to lengthen into claws. The human part of him fought for control. *I gotta get us out of here before he shifts or I do ...*

Ghost curled his lips back from his teeth in a snarl. His face was nearly all bear now. In the dim hallway, with the frightened building residents interested only in getting out, no one was paying much attention—but they'd notice in a hurry if a couple of bears started getting into a knock-down, drag-out fight.

There's no room. If we fight here, we're going to kill someone.

He couldn't drag Ghost out of the hallway, and if he let him up, Ghost would go after Gaby. The only thing he could think to do was to make Ghost so angry he'd forget all about Gaby.

"So you'd rather go after a helpless human than fight me, huh? Did I really beat you that bad in Peru?"

"You *lost* in Peru," Ghost growled.

A quick flare of remembered pain in his scars reminded him how true that was. That fight had bloodied his claws too, though, and he snarled back, "Seems like I remember *you* got torn up pretty bad. Or is that why you've been avoiding me all over this city, because you're scared you'll 'win' again?"

"I'll show *you* how fucking scared I am!"

Ghost's body bucked, humping up with muscle and fur. His clothes tore off him as he shifted, and Derek was flung off. He caught himself and rolled, and came up drawing his gun, but he didn't dare fire. The hallway had mostly emptied out, but there were still a few stragglers. Too much chance he'd hit a civilian.

His plan had worked, though, sort of. Ghost's attention was definitely off Gaby and onto Derek. Except now, he had a pissed-off polar bear after him.

Yay?

Rather than shift in the hallway, he turned and sprinted for the rear exit. He slammed through the exit door and stumbled into the alley behind the apartment building. He'd hoped it would be deserted, but instead there were scattered groups of apartment residents standing around, looking up at the building.

"Get out of here!" Derek yelled at them, waving the gun. He didn't point it at anyone, but the combination of armed, angry, and disheveled worked like a magic charm to get them moving out of the danger zone toward the street.

Just in time, too, as an enraged polar bear slammed into the exit door just as it swung shut.

Derek leveled the gun at him. He still didn't dare shoot until the Ghost was in the alley, because a stray bullet could go straight down the hall and into some hapless grandma. Maybe even into Gaby. He'd rather die than be responsible for hurting her.

For a moment he thought Ghost wasn't going to be able to get through the door without having to shift. Ghost's massive shoulders were too wide. As he angled for a safe shot, finger on the trigger of his gun, all Derek could see in the doorway was a seething mass of yellow-white fur and snarling fangs and small, enraged eyes.

Then Ghost powered through the door on sheer fury, scraping off fur on both shoulders. Derek got off one wild shot before the massive, furious polar bear flattened him.

NOW I'd better shift! He let his bear surge upward as he held Ghost off, both hands clutched on the fur under Ghost's chin. The bear's strength, added to his own, gave him that extra bit of muscle to keep Ghost from ripping his throat out as he felt his own body start to change—

Something slammed into Ghost and suddenly the bear was no longer on top of him, rolling end over end across the alley to slam into the wall.

There was a screech of brakes.

Dazed, Derek stared up at the bumper of his own car, inches from him.

The car ... had hit the bear?

The driver's door cracked open and Gaby leaned out. "Derek! Get in!"

Derek scrambled to his feet, curling his hands to force his claws back into normal human fingertips. His bear snarled inside him as he fought it down. But this wasn't the time or place for a bear fight. Too many possible witnesses. Too much potential for someone to get hurt.

Too much potential for Gaby to get hurt, since she plainly wasn't going to stay out of it.

As he piled into the passenger seat, he snapped, "I told you to leave!"

"Not without you!" Gaby shot back, though she looked terrified. She stamped her foot on the gas pedal, sending the car roaring out of the alley. Looking back, Derek saw the polar bear struggling to get up.

"Gabriella dear, did you just hit a bear with this man's car?" Luisa said from the backseat.

"That was awesome, Mom!" Sandy crowed. "Do it again!"

GABY

She couldn't believe she'd just hit a friggin' *bear* with a Mustang. At least Derek's car was an older model, built back when cars were made of heavy steel, before all the concern about crumple zones and fuel efficiency. A modern car probably wouldn't have survived. She'd felt the shock all through the frame when they hit him, and it looked like the front end was a little bit crumpled, but the car was still driving just fine as Gaby skidded out onto the street, nearly getting run over by a delivery van that honked loudly at her.

"Slow down," Derek panted. "He can't chase us on foot when we're in a car."

Gaby forced herself to slow to something approaching the speed limit. Her hands were shaking. She'd just fled a burning building, got attacked by an assassin, and hit a polar bear with someone else's car.

She glanced sideways at Derek. There was blood all over his shoulder. "Do—do you need a hospital?"

"I'll live," he said. "Take us to the hotel."

"But you're bleeding—"

"It's more important to get you somewhere safe."

"You just got mauled by a polar bear!"

"I'll heal."

From the backseat, Luisa remarked approvingly, "He's as stubborn as you are. Good match for you."

"Mama! I can't believe you're matchmaking at a time like this!" Looking up, she registered a light turning red, slammed on the brakes and skidded to a halt with the car's nose in the crosswalk. The car behind her honked. "Yeah, I'd like to see you do better after the day I've had, buddy!" she yelled over her shoulder.

"Gabriella," her mother said disapprovingly. "You are driving like a maniac."

"Mother, if you can do better, you are very welcome to come up and take the wheel." Gaby huffed out her breath, blowing a loose strand of hair off her nose. "Derek, I have no idea where I'm going."

"Hotel," Derek said. Grimacing, he reached across his body to holster the gun he was still holding, and then fumbled in his pocket. "Do you remember where it is?"

"Yes, sort of, but is it safe?" She still couldn't believe Ghost had set fire to the apartment building just to get to her. She craned at the rear-view, trying to see if there was a plume of smoke. The city skyline appeared undisturbed.

Derek got his phone out one-handed. "Safe enough. I don't think he knows about the hotel."

"Yes, but if he did that once—" Gaby swallowed, looking in the rear-view mirror again.

"The light is green, Gabriella," her mother said helpfully.

"I *know*, Mama!" she snapped, stomping on the gas.

"Your apartment should be okay, Gaby," Derek said, seeming to read her thoughts. "The fire department got there quickly, and it wasn't a big fire to begin with. He just needed the fire alarms to go off. And there'll be better security at the hotel. He won't just be able to walk in."

"Yes, but—" Gaby clenched her teeth on a protest. She was all too close to tears, and she wasn't about to break down in front of her son.

"You're holding up great," Derek told her quietly. "I'm gonna call Keegan and get some extra cops on the hotel, okay?"

Wordlessly, Gaby nodded. Derek put the phone to his ear.

"Keegan? Meet me at the hotel. Bring a first-aid kit. Oh, and a change of clothes would be good, too."

Gaby couldn't hear the words, but she was able to hear the exasperated tone on the other end of the line.

"*I* didn't do anything to *myself*," Derek said, sounding annoyed. "We had a little encounter with the Ghost at Gab— at Diaz's place. We're gonna need to beef up security on the hotel."

Gaby tried to tune out the conversation as the two of them started hashing out details. When she stopped at the next traffic light, she twisted around to look into the back-seat and forced a smile. "How are you two doing back here? Sandy, are you taking care of Grandma like I told you to?"

Luisa smiled and put an arm around her grandson. "He's doing very well."

Sandy nodded, his curls bouncing. "Mom, you ran over a *bear*."

"Pretty exciting day, huh?"

"Yes," Sandy agreed. "I'm hungry."

That's right, dinner was cooling and congealing on their table. "We'll get dinner where we're going," Gaby told him. "We're eating out tonight. That'll be cool, right?"

"The light is green, Gabriella."

"I know," Gaby sighed, putting the car in gear.

~

S he parked in the underground garage. Derek took the backpack and Gaby helped her mother unfold the walker for the trek upstairs.

"Keegan's looking into getting a second room on the same floor, so we won't be crammed into one," Derek said.

Normally she'd have been delighted to have some alone time with Derek, but right now she just wanted the whole family together, where she could keep an eye on them. Still, Derek's vigilance as he shepherded them upstairs made her feel a little safer.

It was impossible to be truly terrified with Derek there. He would keep her safe. Even against someone who could turn into a polar bear.

She remembered the solid impact as the car's bumper connected with the Ghost. That was the moment when he'd stopped feeling like an apparition and started feeling truly real, and somehow, that actually made it better. He might be a monster, but he wasn't *really* a ghost. He could be hurt. He could be stopped.

Does Derek ... turn into something like that?

She wished she could talk to him about it, without her mother and Sandy present. Okay, maybe separate rooms were going to be a plus.

But for now, they all crowded into the room where she and Derek had eaten lunch—and done a few other things, she realized with a shock of embarrassed horror at the sight of the rumpled bed. Hastily she flipped the covers up over the sheets, and then, for good measure, sat on them to make sure her mother didn't choose that bed to sit on.

She needn't have worried; Luisa took the chair, parking her walker next to it.

"So what's our next move?" Gaby asked.

"Food?" Sandy suggested hopefully, climbing into her lap.

"Food sounds good," Derek said. He handed the room service menu to her. "Order me a steak. Don't worry about cost; you aren't paying. I'm just gonna go in the bathroom and get cleaned up. Don't open the front door unless you're sure of who it is."

As the bathroom door closed behind him, Gaby wished she knew how bad his injuries really were. He was moving almost normally, but his shirt was tattered and bloody around the shoulder.

She tried to take her mind off it by helping Sandy pick out something from the menu, followed by arguing with her mother over it. Luisa insisted on picking the cheapest item she could find. "Mama, no. Order what you like. If we're going to have to go through all of this, you should at least get a good dinner out of it."

Just as Gaby was hanging up the phone after placing their order, someone knocked on the door. Luisa started to struggle out of her chair to answer it.

"Mama, no! It's too soon to be our food." Gaby put her arms around Sandy. *Could he have found us so soon?*

Derek came swiftly from the bathroom, stripped to the waist, with a towel flung over his injured shoulder and his gun in one hand. Gaby wished terror weren't interfering with her appreciation of all the naked, toned manflesh on display.

"There's someone at the door," she said, trying to keep her voice from shaking.

"I know." Derek glanced through the peephole, sighed, and opened the door. "You're gonna get shot doing that, Keegan."

"You were expecting me," Keegan retorted, shoving a bundled-up bag in Derek's direction. "Ms. Diaz. Shame we couldn't meet again under better circumstances. This is your family, I presume?"

Introductions went around, while Derek vanished back into the bathroom. Gaby left her mother talking to Keegan, and went to tap on the bathroom door. "Derek?" she called quietly. "Do you need any help?"

After a pause, Derek said, "C'mon in. Just you."

Gaby slipped through the door and closed it behind her. Derek was sitting on the closed lid of the toilet. The bag that Keegan had brought was open on the counter, with gauze and other first-aid supplies scattered around, along with a balled-up, clean shirt.

The towel was no longer covering his shoulder, so she got her first good look at the damage Ghost had done. No wonder he'd been trying not to use his left arm. His shoulder was a mass of clotted blood and the yellowish stain of iodine smeared around puncture wounds. Gaby tried not to let her horror show on her face, but from Derek's wry, tired smile, she didn't think she'd managed.

"It's not as bad as it looks."

"It looks pretty bad! You shouldn't be patching it up yourself. You need antibiotics! Stitches! We have to get you to an emergency room."

Derek shook his head. "Shifters heal fast. It'll be almost good as new in a day or two."

"Are you serious?"

He nodded, then winced as the movement pulled at the wounds. "I just need to get it cleaned up so my body won't have to work as hard to heal it. I've done the front, but it'd be really great to get someone else to help me with the back."

"Oh no, there's more?"

"The front's the worst," Derek said. Gritting his teeth, he leaned forward.

"Well, I hope so, because if your back is worse than this,

I'm getting the lieutenant to help me drag you off to a hospital whether you want to go or not."

But he was right; his back was much less damaged, mostly scraped and bruised. As she leaned over his shoulder, cleaning the injuries while he bore it in stoic silence, Gaby tried to focus on her task and not on the muscles of his back, the graceful curve of his spine. Or on how good his hair smelled, an intensely masculine smell ...

As a mom, she had more than her share of experience at cleaning up minor injuries, and she was fascinated to see that the scrapes on his back looked like they were already starting to heal up. They certainly didn't look like they'd been made no more than an hour ago.

Which made her wonder about the scars on his side. If shifters healed as fast as he said, how bad had *those* wounds been, to leave scars like that?

"You doing okay?" Derek asked quietly. His voice was a low rumble; leaning over his shoulder, half in his lap, she could feel the vibration through his rib cage.

"I am. So far. Having to keep it together for Mama and Sandy actually helps in a way, you know? If it was just me, I'd probably be a basket case by now."

"I find that hard to believe," Derek murmured. "You're brave and tough, Gaby. Hell, you probably saved my life today."

She could feel herself blushing and turned her face away as she finished disinfecting his scrapes. "Well, the only reason why you're here at all is because you're protecting me. I couldn't just run off without trying to help."

"A lot of people would have."

She couldn't think of anything to say, especially not with all of him in such close proximity to her. She turned her head just as he turned his, and his lips met hers, warm and soft.

"Gabriella!" her mother called through the door. "The food is here!"

They smiled against each others' lips. "Duty calls," Gaby murmured.

"We'll have to pick up where we left off a little later."

"I'm looking forward to it."

He nibbled her bottom lip lightly and then let go. With reluctance, she pulled away and washed her hands in the sink while Derek, wincing slightly, put on the clean shirt.

"Do I look like I was just fighting a bear?"

"No, you look great—oh, wait." She stood on tiptoe to kiss him again, and carefully folded down the collar of the shirt. "Okay, *now* you look great."

"I'm glad it meets your exacting standards," he said dryly, and opened the door.

The food smelled wonderful, making Gaby's stomach grumble and reminding her how long it had been since she'd last put anything in it. She'd expected Lt. Keegan to be gone, but he was still there, sitting on a corner of the neatly made-up bed with one leg tucked under him.

"Get us another hotel room yet?" Derek asked him.

"Actually, I've got a better idea." Keegan reached into his pocket and took out something that rattled. He tossed it to Derek, and Gaby saw that it was a set of keys. "I have a cabin out in the sticks, north of the city. Nobody knows about it, and it's not even in my name. It's for the times when I need to get off the grid for a little while."

"But—" Gaby began. "My job, my classes—"

"It could be your job or your life," Keegan said. "Is it worth it for a minimum wage job pulling coffee shots?"

"It's not about that," Gaby snapped. "It's about providing for my family and building a better life for them and myself."

"Gaby." Derek gently turned her to face him. "I get where you're coming from, believe me, but I think it's time to start considering that you might need to get out of the city for a little while. If nothing else, think about your boss and the other people you work with. If the Ghost comes for you, everyone at the coffee shop will be in danger."

Gaby sighed and buried her hands in her hair.

"He's right, Gabriella," her mother said softly.

And that was the worst part: they *were* right. After what had happened at her apartment building, she couldn't go on justifying putting the people around her in danger to hang onto her old life.

It's temporary, she promised herself, and got out her phone to call Polly.

Polly was nothing but sympathetic. "I thought you might make that decision. I've already got someone lined up to help with the morning shift tomorrow."

"You're the best," Gaby said, relieved. "But this won't be for long, I swear. Only until this situation is dealt with."

"Just stay safe," Polly told her.

As Gaby hung up, she looked at her family. Sandy was in Luisa's lap, eating chicken nuggets off the edge of Luisa's plate.

We'll ALL be safe, she thought firmly. *Or, so help me, I'm making a polar bear skin rug out of that bastard.*

DEREK

I t was the darkest and coldest part of the night when Derek pulled up in front of Keegan's cabin, or at least, the most likely candidate to be the right cabin, based on the vague directions Keegan had given him. They'd wound their way down little country roads, leaving the last town behind and driving up into the mountains. The turnoff to the actual driveway (if you could call it that) was marked only with a dab of reflective orange paint on a tree.

Derek knew Keegan was private, but he'd never realized the guy liked his privacy quite *this* much.

Still, as the Mustang's headlights swept across the dark cabin, Derek relaxed a little. He knew they hadn't been followed—on these rural roads, it would have been obvious —so the only way anyone could find them was if they got the address out of Keegan, which wasn't likely. Nowhere in the city felt safe, not with Ghost on the hunt. Out here, Derek felt like they'd gained a little breathing room.

The problem was, if Ghost *did* find them, help would be hours away and there was nowhere to run except the woods.

Yeah, but the woods are where I'm most at home. Bring it, asshole.

He killed the engine and glanced over at Gaby in the passenger seat. It was almost completely dark, the only light shed by the cold bright points of the stars overhead, but with his shifter-enhanced night vision, he could just barely glimpse her tired smile. She'd been quiet for most of the drive—worn out, he thought, as the incredibly busy and exhausting day had finally caught up with her. Still, every time he'd glanced over at her, she had been awake, gazing out at the dark scenery.

"Ready to get some shut-eye?" he asked her quietly.

"I guess so. I'm not really sleepy." Then she belied her own words with a sudden yawn. "Okay, maybe I am. Mama, are you awake back there?"

"Wide awake, dear. But our little one has been out for hours."

Derek glanced into the backseat. Sandy was fast asleep, lying down with his head in Luisa's lap.

"It looks like there are steps up to the cabin porch, Mama," Gabriella said. "I can help you with your walker."

"Oh, heavens, my heart. I can handle a couple of steps."

"For the moment, you should all stay here," Derek told them. "I'm just going to look around first."

Gaby made a hurt noise. "Oh, I'm so *tired* of this." There was a world of exhaustion in her voice that made Derek want to take her in his arms and shield her from the world.

And it also made him want to say, *If you think you're tired now, wait until you've been on the run for weeks or months.* But she didn't know what that was like. And he didn't ever want her to know. If this was the most pain and terror that Gaby Diaz ever felt, then he would have done his job. He wished she'd never even had to feel this much, but all he could do was go ahead and try to keep her safe from here on out.

He left Gaby and her family in the car, and climbed onto the cabin's porch, gun in hand, all his senses alert. The healing injury tugged beneath his shirt, reminding him of the steep price that a lack of caution could bring.

But he had no sense of danger here. When he inhaled the night air, letting his bear close enough to the surface to sharpen his sense of smell, all he could detect were the scents of pine trees, grass, and the Mustang's cooling engine. He heard nothing to alarm him. There had been no other recent car tracks on the driveway.

The door opened easily at a turn of Keegan's key, and Derek flicked on the lights, showing him a small, comfortable living room with exposed wooden beams and overstuffed furniture. There was no TV, but there were shelves of paperback novels and a small fireplace with a stone hearth.

It was a nice little retreat from the world. He could see why Keegan liked it up here.

The cabin was small enough that he could explore it in a few minutes. There were two downstairs bedrooms, a bathroom, and a small kitchen nook. The upstairs was nothing more than a loft with another bedroom and some storage space. Everything was neat and tidy. The beds were stripped down to bare mattresses, but he found plenty of sheets and pillows. There was no sign anyone had been in here. When he tested the cabin's phone, he got a dial tone, although a quick check of his cell phone showed no reception. They would be dependent on the land line to communicate with the outside world.

Coming out onto the porch, he was annoyed to find Gaby getting her family's things out of the trunk. "I told you to stay in the car," he said, holstering the gun as he loped over to her.

"It's safe here, though, isn't it?" she said. "I can tell by the way you're acting. You were very different at the hotel."

Was he? The idea that she could read him so easily made

something twist in his chest. It had been a very long time since he'd allowed anyone to know him so well. Perhaps no one ever had.

"Yeah, it's safe," he said. "You still should have stayed in the car."

"I'm allowed to make my own judgment calls some of the time. Or didn't you mean what you said at the hotel, about me being brave?"

Stubborn mate. She was definitely a woman who could go head-to-head with an equally stubborn bear ... but of course, as his mate, she'd have to be. "Yeah, you are. But this is my area of expertise, all right?"

Gaby paused and looked up at him, her eyes glimmering in the starlight. "All right," she said solemnly. "You're right. When it comes to personal safety, I'll do as you say. But ..." Now he caught a glimmer of a teasing smile. "In *my* areas of expertise, you have to do what *I* say."

"I thought we established that at the coffee shop."

"Yes, we did, didn't we?" She slid an arm around his waist and stretched on tiptoe to give him a quick peck on the lips. "My big, bad barista."

The car door opened, making Gaby jump. "Why doesn't your big, bad barista put those big, nicely muscled arms to good use," Luisa suggested, "and carry your sleeping son into the house?"

"Mama!"

"I'd be happy to," Derek said.

Luisa handed the limp, fast-asleep child out of the back-seat, into his arms. Derek stood still for a moment, stunned by the small, yet oddly dense weight against his chest. The child was heavier than he had expected for something so tiny, though of course not even approaching difficult for him to pick up.

Or maybe it was only the weight of all that potential that

felt so heavy, all those not-yet-fulfilled expectations that went along with being a child.

And these people trusted *him*, with his scarred and blood-stained hands, to hold this child?

It was the closest he'd come so far to thinking *I can't do this*.

But his mate was standing beside him, looking up at him with eyes that held nothing but trust and love.

"Get the door?" he asked her gruffly, and she nodded.

Carefully, acutely aware of the precious burden he carried, he climbed the steps to the porch with Sandy's curly, sleeping head resting against his chest. Gaby opened the door for him, and then hurried back down to give her mother a hand up the steps.

Derek realized once he was inside that he hadn't told her the beds weren't made. He laid Sandy carefully on the couch; the child squirmed, pressed his face into the couch cushions, and went back to sleep. Derek got out an armload of bedding and started making the beds.

"He makes beds too!" came Luisa's approving voice from the doorway, followed instantly by the now-familiar, exasperated exclamation of "*Mother!*" from further away; Gaby seemed to be out in the kitchen area somewhere.

Luisa, however, came into the bedroom, moving carefully with her walker, which she pushed against the wall. With sharp eyes, she watched Derek tuck the sheet under the edge of the bed in crisp, military-neat corners, and gave a brief, satisfied nod.

"Gimme a hand with those blankets?" Derek asked.

Between the two of them, they pulled a blanket tight across the bed, and Derek held the pillows while Luisa slipped on their cases. "It's always easier with two," she remarked. "I used to do housework with Gaby like this, when she was a girl."

"It was just the two of you?"

"For a good long time, it was." A flicker of a very deep and very old sorrow crossed her face, but then it was chased away by a slightly wistful smile. "And it's just been *you* for a very long time, I'd guess."

"You'd be right about that, ma'am." He hesitated. "Want to help me fix up the other bedroom?"

"I'd love to." Luisa plumped the pillows and limped out of the room after him, leaving the walker behind.

"So tell me about your parents," she said as they worked together to fix the bed in the other bedroom. "Still alive?"

"Both dead. My grandparents raised me. They're dead now, too. No siblings." Derek smiled briefly as he reached for the pillows. "Is this the kind of interview you give your daughter's bodyguard, or—"

"Or the man my daughter might be dating? No need to look guilty about it. I've been hoping for years that Gaby will think about herself once in awhile, rather than always putting other people first as she does. She needs to find a nice man, I tell her."

"And am I, you think?" Derek asked quietly, looking down at his hands on the pillows. Big hands, browned by the sun, callused from handling guns and knives.

"If I didn't think you were a good man, you would know it," Luisa said, just as quietly. "I wouldn't have a bad man in my house, at my dinner table."

"You've only known me for a few hours."

"Yes, and so? The first time I ever spoke to Gaby's father, I said to myself, Luisa, that is the man you are going to marry. And I did."

Did humans have fated mates, too? Derek had never really considered it. Gaby certainly seemed to feel the same longing and trust for him that he felt for her.

"Make my daughter happy, Derek," Luisa said softly. "Protect her. Take care of her every day of her life."

"Trust me, ma'am, that's all I want to do."

Luisa smiled. "And that is all I need to hear. Now, if you'll excuse me, I'm an old woman and I am going to bed. You can put Alejo in the other bedroom downstairs, so I will hear him if he needs anything in the night. And you and Gaby can take the upstairs bedroom."

"Good night, ma'am," Derek told her. Feeling slightly dazed, he went out to the living room and picked Sandy up carefully off the couch.

Gaby was looking at the spines of the books on the shelves lining the walls. She looked up quickly and gave him a smile, then followed him into the bedroom and pulled the covers down. Derek laid Sandy carefully on the bed. Gaby slipped his shoes off, pulled the covers up, and leaned over to kiss his forehead.

Quietly, shutting the lights off behind them, they went back out to the living room. The door to Luisa's bedroom was closed.

"Front door is locked, right?" Derek asked. Gaby nodded. "It looks like your mother has assigned our bedrooms. I hope you're okay with the upstairs one."

"Of course I am, and of course she has," Gaby sighed. "I hope she didn't ask you too many embarrassing questions. I once caught her asking my prom date about his masturbation habits. The poor kid was mortified."

"She's looking out for you, though. You're lucky to have her."

"I know. It's just ..." She lowered her voice and said with a slight smile, "Sometimes I wish there was a little *less* of her. I love my mom, but sharing a two-bedroom apartment with her can really be a lot of mom."

"Well, she's tucked safely in bed now, so you want to see what the upstairs bedroom is like?"

It was actually the one Derek would've chosen for himself anyway. He had a feeling this was probably where Keegan stayed when he was at the cabin. Panthers liked to be up high. Derek didn't have that urge in general, but he liked the way the bedroom's several small windows looked out onto the woods.

Gaby was the one who pointed out a trap door in the ceiling, while Derek fixed the bed. "Where does that go?"

"Attic, probably."

But it wasn't an attic. When they climbed up the fold-down ladder, they found a little cupola on top of the roof, just big enough to accommodate the two of them, and just tall enough for Derek to stand up straight. There was a bench built into the wall, and windows all around. If the bedroom had offered a nice view of the woods, this observation tower—and Derek had no doubt that was what it was—took it up a notch. From up here, you could see anyone approaching the cabin from any direction. He looked down at the Mustang parked in front of the cabin, the woodshed beside it, and the dark sea of the woods sloping down to distant neighbors' lights.

"I'm not sure what to think about this Keegan guy," Gaby murmured. She slid an arm around Derek's waist. "I almost feel like I'm in a sniper nest. Ex-military, is he?"

"He's actually an engineer, believe it or not."

Gaby laughed. "They don't make engineers like that at *my* school."

The reminder that she was going to school made him think, again, about the vast gulf in life experience between the two of them. It wasn't that much of a difference in age. She was at least in her mid-20s, only a few years younger than he was. But he'd gone places, seen things, *done* things that he couldn't expect her to understand.

And yet ...

She'd done things he hadn't, either. She was raising her son on her own, and supporting a disabled mother at the same time. And if he knew her at all, he knew that she did it quietly and uncomplainingly, day after day.

"Penny for your thoughts," Gaby said, leaning her head against his chest.

"Just thinking we might not be that different, after all."

She laughed incredulously. "I've seen those scars you have. You keep telling me I'm brave, but—"

"It's not a lie." He tilted her head back with a finger on her chin, and lightly sampled her sweet lips. "Not many people would've been able to do what you did. Not many people could do what you do every day."

"What, go to work at a coffee shop?"

"And come home, take care of your son and mother, and take classes so you can work your way to a better life for them. No, Gaby, not many people could do that."

"I keep feeling like you've built me up in your head to be this amazing person, and you're going to get to know me and be disappointed."

"Trust me, Gaby." He kissed her again, lightly sipping at her full lips. "Nothing about you could ever be boring to me."

Their soft kisses turned heated and passionate. Fire blazed through him, igniting at her touch. No one he'd ever known had been able to get this kind of response from him. Gaby did it as easily as breathing. And part of the reason for that was how genuine and honest she was. Gaby was completely and utterly herself, every minute of the day.

Part of it, of course, was that she was his mate, and he would always burn for his mate's touch. He'd been yearning for it since long before he knew she existed.

But it was also Gaby, the whole enticing package of her. He loved her soul and he loved her mind. She was kind and smart and fun to talk to. The heat that burned in him could not have blazed so brightly for anyone else on Earth.

He cupped his hands under her enticing buttocks. She gasped against his mouth and thrust her hips against him, pushing her crotch into his burgeoning erection.

"I don't know about you," she murmured, biting at his lip, "but *I'm* sure ready for round two. And unless that's something else in your pocket, I think you are too."

"Mmmm. The only thing I have in my pocket is for you." He winced. "Okay, that wasn't my best-ever attempt at dirty talk."

"How about this?" She looped her arms around his neck and leaned close to murmur into his ear, in a husky whisper, "I want you to lay me back on these bench cushions and fuck me 'til I go out of my mind."

His cock registered enthusiastic approval. "You win," he said hoarsely. "The dirty talking award goes to Gabriella Diaz. But let's do it downstairs. I don't want to risk kicking out a window or falling through the trapdoor."

Also, it didn't seem like good houseguest behavior without at least bringing up a blanket to throw over the bench seat. He filed it away for a future possibility, though. Making love up here would be like making love among the stars.

He climbed down the ladder in a few quick hops, just in time to get a lovely view of Gaby's round hips and delicious thighs as she descended after him. Derek caught her around the waist before she'd reached the floor and swept her off the ladder. Gaby's initial squeal of laughter was quickly muffled behind her hand, reminding Derek that they had to be quiet to avoid waking the household. Rather than collapsing onto the bed with her as he'd planned, he laid her down gently, while Gaby's eyes sparkled at him.

So they'd have to be quiet. He could do that. He grinned back at her, and started undoing the fastening on her jeans.

He stripped her one item of clothing at a time, kissing his way along each newly bared bit of skin. He nipped at her collar-bone, kissed his way across the soft curve of her belly, licked at her dark brown nipples. He could smell her growing arousal, and hear it in the soft noises she made, especially when he buried his face in the curls between her legs and tasted her salt.

When he finally entered her, she was hot and ready. She rose to meet him, wrapping her legs around him, meeting each of his thrusts with an eager surge of her hips.

He felt her shudder into the first throes of her climax, and that sent him over the edge, filling her with his heat until they sank down together, spent and pleasantly relaxed.

"I'm going to sleep well tonight, I think," Gaby murmured.

"Same." He wasn't worried about needing to stand watch. The cabin door was locked, and he knew his bear would rouse him at the first hint of trouble. But he really didn't think they'd been followed. For a little while, at least, they could relax.

And he really felt like he *could* relax. There was none of the tension that usually heralded a night full of bad dreams. Just a lazy, pleasant lassitude, and comfort in the presence of his mate.

After a moment he became aware of Gaby squirming, leaning off the bed and feeling for something on the floor. He made a questioning noise.

"Just trying to find my underwear. Ah. Here it is." She sat up and swung her legs off the bed to put it on. "I'd prefer not to sleep naked. If it was just the two of us, sure, but ..."

"Yeah, I get it." He sat up and hunted around for his briefs.

"I don't suppose you've got a spare T-shirt I can sleep in, do you?"

"I don't, but I bet Keegan does." He found a couple of clean T-shirts in the closet, one with a gym logo, the other with the name of a truck stop on it, and held them up. "Take your pick."

"Oh ... that one, I guess." She pointed to the truck stop one. "Poor Keegan. I feel like a bizarre modern version of Goldilocks. Sleeping in his bed ..." She pulled the T-shirt over her head. It was tight over her breasts and much too large everywhere else. "Wearing his clothes ..."

"It's okay. We'll just tidy up before we leave. Ready to sleep?"

Gaby nodded. Derek flicked off the light, plunging the room into the true darkness that you never got in the city. There was always some light, even with the blinds closed.

He didn't really need darkness to sleep. He'd gotten used to being able to fall asleep anytime, anywhere. But there was something peaceful and comforting, very soothing to his bear, about this complete darkness with no sign of artificial light anywhere.

Yeah. He knew why Keegan liked it up here.

He made his way back to the bed by feel and curled up against Gaby, burying his nose in her neck and inhaling the scent of woman and sex and *mate*.

Tomorrow he might have to fight, but tonight he was truly and utterly content.

He sank into sleep, and didn't dream once.

GABY

G aby woke to sunlight spilling across her pillow.
She almost never got to sleep in. *I overslept,* she thought dazedly. *My morning shift—I'm going to be late—*

Then she registered that, first of all, this wasn't her bed. Second, she was alone in the bed, which she hadn't been when she'd fallen asleep, and she could hear voices and laughter coming from downstairs.

Gaby sat up and yawned, her hair falling messily in her face. She pushed a handful out of the way so she could see, and sat up. She was wearing nothing except yesterday's underwear and an oversized T-shirt that belonged to Keegan.

I should've had Derek take us back to the apartment so we could get a change of clothes. Then she remembered her last sight of her apartment building and shivered. *If the apartment is even still there ...*

But she thought Derek was right that her apartment probably hadn't been harmed. All they'd have to do was clean up a congealed casserole dish when they got home, at the end of all of this.

Please, for all our sakes, let this be over soon.

Another burst of high-pitched childish giggling came from downstairs, and Gaby decided it was time to figure out what was going on down there. Also, she could smell coffee and the delicious smell of something frying, which made her realize that she was starving. Dinner at the hotel had been a long time ago.

She climbed into yesterday's clothes. A hairbrush, apparently, was yet another thing she hadn't packed, so she combed her hair with her fingers, and then stepped out to the railing of the loft, looking down in the cabin's living room.

Everyone else was already up. Luisa was on the couch with a cup of coffee. Derek and Sandy were in the kitchen; she had to lean out farther to see them. There was a griddle on the stove, a bowl of batter beside it, and a plate with a stack of odd-shaped pancakes on it.

Derek, making pancakes. Her head swam at the mental incongruity.

"What do you want this one to look like?" Derek asked Sandy, dribbling batter onto the griddle.

"Ummm ... a puppy!"

"The last one was a puppy. How about something different this time?"

"Ummmm," Sandy said, bouncing on his toes.

"How about an elephant?" Derek suggested.

"Can you make a pancake ephelant?" Sandy sounded incredulous.

"Sure you can." Derek began carefully pouring batter from a cup. "See, here's the body ... it's got to be bigger than the other pancakes, of course ... and we can do the trunk like this ... would you like to make the legs?"

"Sure!" Sandy crowed, holding his arms up in the air.

Derek handed him the cup of batter and then picked him

up. Gaby had to force herself to squash a surge of parental warnings, such as *Don't hold him too close to the hot grease!* and *He's going to drip! You have to guide his hand!*

But they seemed to be doing just fine. Against all odds, Derek Ruger, badass and professional bodyguard, appeared to be good with kids.

Gaby padded quietly down the stairs, not wanting to disturb them. Her mother noticed her and held out an arm. Gaby came over to receive a good-morning hug and kissed her mother on top of the head. Despite the lack of amenities, Luisa had somehow managed to get her hair brushed perfectly smooth and pinned up with the combs she'd been wearing yesterday.

"There's food here?"

"Some," Luisa said, smiling. "We found pancake mix and a sealed bottle of syrup in one of the cabinets. Derek says that his friend would not mind."

"Well, he did say we could use the cabin. I guess he wouldn't expect us to starve here." She made a mental note to do something nice for Derek's friend Keegan. Send him a thank-you card at the very least. She also filed away the mental note that apparently her mother and Derek were on a first-name basis now.

Derek looked around and saw her, and broke into a beaming smile that sent a pleasant shiver through her middle. "Hey, look who's up. Sandy, it's your momma."

"Mom!" Sandy cried happily. "Look, I'm making pancakes!"

In his excitement, he waved his arms and nearly poured batter down Derek's collar. Gaby hurried to rescue the batter cup before it spilled.

"Uh, thanks." Derek grinned ruefully. "We're doing pretty well at not getting it everywhere. Only a few drops so far."

"You should see what the kitchen looks like after a pancake breakfast at home. Trust me, you're doing *great*."

"I made an ephelant!" Sandy said.

"It's the best elephant I've ever seen. And I have seen a few elephants in my time," she said, winking at Derek.

"When?" Sandy asked, round-eyed.

"Well, last year at the zoo, for one. Do you remember that?"

"Ummmm."

"With the flamingos?" He'd been very impressed by the flamingos, she recalled.

"Oooh." His small brow cleared. "Oh, yeah."

"Anyone ready to eat?" Derek asked, setting a plate of pancakes onto the table with a flourish.

For a little while, the only sounds were those of four people industriously eating, with an occasional "Please pass the syrup" or "May I have some more?" Gaby tucked away three pancakes single-handedly, but that was nothing compared to the stack that Derek inhaled.

"A man who is a good eater is also a good provider," Luisa declared approvingly.

Gaby stifled her semi-instinctive urge to sigh, and leaned over to Sandy. "Regardless of what your grandma says, a grown-up lady doesn't need a man to buy her things."

"Perhaps not," Luisa said, "but it is a very nice thing to have."

"Mama ... please ..."

After breakfast, Luisa insisted on doing the cleanup, with Sandy "helping." Derek and Gaby went out on the porch. The morning was crisp and clean, with the sun peeking through scattered clouds, just enough to knock the edge off the heat and make the day pleasant.

"I took a walk around this morning, before everyone else was up," Derek said quietly. "Scouted around the cabin and walked a little way down the driveway. Absolutely no sign of anyone coming to bother us. We're all alone up here."

"I really appreciate that. I just wish I knew how long this was going to keep up."

"You want my advice?" Derek asked, tweaking a dark strand of hair off her shoulder.

"I'll take any advice you want to give."

"Relax. Enjoy it. When was the last time you had a vacation?"

"This isn't a vacation, though. This is hiding out in the middle of nowhere, while a killer stalks me."

He put his arms around her and slowly rocked her, pressing a kiss to the top of her head. "Look around you. I won't lie, you've been through some rough stuff, but this looks like paradise on Earth to me."

Gradually, a little at a time, Gaby let herself relax into the gentle swaying. It was utterly quiet here, the quietest place she'd ever been. She kept expecting to hear traffic noises, but the only traffic was an occasional distant car on the highway, so faint she had to strain to hear it. She could hear individual birds singing in the woods, and a gentle rushing sound that might have been wind or water.

"There's a spring behind the house," Derek said, speaking as if in response to her thoughts—she couldn't get over the way he could do that. "It's not deep enough to be dangerous. Your son might enjoy playing in the water a little later."

"You can't read my mind, can you?"

"What?"

"You're all but finishing my sentences already. Even Mama and I can hardly do that."

"Oh. That." He rocked her slowly in silence before speaking again. "It's not telepathy, not exactly. It's just that, as mates, we're very in tune with each other. I could see that you were listening, so I thought you might want me to explain what you were hearing." He cocked his head. "That's a robin singing, by the way."

"You promise you're not using actual telepathy? You'd tell me if you were?"

Derek laughed. "I promise. The only thing I can do is turn into a bear."

She tipped back her head to smile up into his face. "I'd love to see that."

"Me as a bear?"

"Yes, you as a bear. Why, don't you want to?"

Derek hesitated and glanced at the house. Then he smiled. "Sure. Why not."

They walked away from the porch and around the corner of the cabin, hand in hand. Behind the cabin, the grass sloped down to a steep little bank and, as Derek had said, a small, rushing stream. He was right; it wasn't more than a few inches deep, just enough to add a picturesque element to the yard.

There was a trail along the edge of the spring, narrow enough that they had to go single file as they walked into the woods.

"I don't want to go too far," Gaby said, glancing back anxiously.

"I know. Me neither. This should be far enough. I just want to make sure we aren't seen from the house."

He was wearing a new T-shirt today, probably another of Keegan's. He stripped it off with only a hint of stiffness this time, and Gaby couldn't help staring at the puckered pink skin where his shoulder looked like it had been healing for a week instead of less than a day.

"You weren't kidding about the fast healing."

"Nope." He took off his holster and started to put it on top of the folded T-shirt, then stopped. "Do you know how to use a gun?"

Gaby shook her head.

"You'd better learn the basics, then."

As he drew the gun from its holster, she shook her head more vigorously. "I don't want to know how. There's no reason why I need to know, not with you here."

"What if something happens to me? You have to be able to protect your son and your mother, if you need to." He expertly disconnected the bullet-filled clip, dropping it into his hand, and stuck it in his pocket. Then he held the gun pointed at the ground, finger off the trigger. "You might've heard people talk about taking off the safety on a gun before you shoot. However, this is a Glock, which means that it has no safety. If there's a bullet in the chamber, it's ready to fire. I don't normally carry it with a bullet chambered for safety reasons. However, you should never, *ever* assume that it's not. Checking for a chambered bullet is called clearing the weapon, and it's always the first thing you should do if anyone hands you a gun. To do that, you pull back the slide—this part here—and look down the barrel. Do it a couple of times to be sure." He demonstrated. "Now you do it."

Gaby reluctantly accepted the gun as he pressed it into her hands. It felt cold to the touch and heavier than she was expecting. "But what if I—break something, or, I don't know ...?"

"You won't hurt it, and I took the clip out, so it can't hurt you. There are no bullets in it now. Clear the weapon like I showed you."

She did it reluctantly. The slide—the spring-loaded top of the gun—was stiffer than she was expecting, and snapped back into place when she let go.

"Now if there was a clip in the gun, the part with the bullets, you would've just chambered one, and it'd be ready to fire." His big hands closed over hers, and he turned her around, so she was held between his arms with her back against his bare chest. "Go ahead and hold it like you're going to shoot. Important piece of safety information: no matter what you see people on TV doing, never put your finger on the trigger until you're ready to fire." He tapped his finger against the side of the barrel. "Just rest it above the trigger so you can move it down when you're ready."

His hands, big and sure, guided hers into position, and he helped her raise the gun. Her heart beat fast. She could feel the strength in his arms, carefully controlled—a force of nature, guided and aimed, the way he was guiding her hands.

"When you're ready," he murmured into her ear, sending a shiver through her, "go ahead and dry-fire the gun a couple of times. It's not good on it to do that a lot, but a couple times won't hurt, and that'll give you a feel for it. Squeeze the trigger gently; don't tug on it."

She carefully squeezed the trigger. With no bullet in the gun, she wasn't expecting it to do anything, but it made a sharp snap like the pop of a spring-loaded toy, and she jumped.

"Just like that." She could hear the smile in Derek's voice. "Except maybe without the jumping. You'll need to pull the slide back again or else the trigger won't work. If there were bullets in the gun, it'd reset automatically and you could keep firing without having to do that."

She did it twice more, and Derek kissed her ear. "Good. Now you know how to fire a gun. I'd have you do some actual target practice, but we didn't warn anyone back at the house, and all I've got with me is one more spare clip in the car's glove box."

He showed her how to put the clip back into the gun, then holstered it and laid the holster on the T-shirt. Gaby felt jittery from a head rush, partly from having the gun in her hands, and partly from being pressed against his naked chest.

She felt ... *powerful.*

It's an illusion, she reminded herself. Okay, so she knew how to shoot a gun now—sort of. Still, that little gun wasn't going to be able to do much against a full-grown polar bear.

But the one thing that *could* take down a giant polar bear was standing right in front of her, stripping off the rest of his clothes until he was gloriously naked in the morning sun.

She had admired Derek's gorgeous physique every time she'd seen him, but this was transcendental. He *belonged* here, with the sun gilding the curling hair on his chest and leaf shadows flickering over his shoulders when the wind stirred the tree branches. Here in the woods, he was like a primal force of nature, like a young forest god, almost seeming to glow in the sun.

When he met her eyes, though, it was one hundred percent Derek looking back at her, smiling gently. "Ready?"

She nodded, not trusting herself to speak.

There wasn't anything spectacular. No lights or sparks or Hollywood-like special effects. He just *flowed,* from one shape to the other, bending over with fluid grace. It was a man's hands that reached for the forest floor, and a bear's paws that landed there.

Derek was a grizzly bear, his fur a medium brown, lighter on the hump of his shoulders and his spine. In the sunlight, he seemed to glow.

He was huge, but she felt not the slightest trace of fear. Nothing about Derek in either of his shapes could ever frighten her.

"May I?" she asked softly, holding out a hand.

Derek came to her with a slow, measured stride, keeping his head low and his body language as nonthreatening as a huge grizzly was capable of. Gaby pushed her hands deep into the thick, coarse fur around his face. Sensing what he might like, without knowing quite how she knew, she scratched him as she might have scratched a large, furry dog. His eyes half closed in bliss.

Then he shifted back, and suddenly she was cupping his face in her hands, with her fingertips pressed to his morning stubble and his naked body nearly touching hers. Gaby let out a small gasp.

"Sorry," he said, grinning down at her. He didn't look sorry in the slightest.

"Flirt," she murmured, and savored a long, gentle kiss.

In his naked state, the stirrings of interest against her hip were all too obvious. Derek broke the kiss to grin at her ruefully. "You know, under other circumstances I'd want to lay you down right here by the spring, in the sunshine, but today ..."

"We should be getting back to the cabin," she sighed.

"Afraid so. We've been gone long enough."

She sat on a log and watched him dress, enjoying the ripple of his muscles and his animal-like grace. It felt so peaceful here, as if Ghost was a whole world away. For the first time in days, she wasn't afraid. She knew that the feeling of safety could turn out to be an illusion. Ghost still might find them here. But right now, with the morning sunshine warm on her hair, it seemed impossible that anything could disturb the tranquility of this place.

The scars on Derek's side were a reminder, though, of the violence that could intrude on their lives at any time, in any place.

"So what happened with you and Ghost, anyway?" she asked. "He sure does seem to have it in for you."

Derek grimaced as he reached for his T-shirt. "I guess you could call it a professional difference of opinion. At least in the beginning."

"How so?"

Derek pulled the shirt over his head. As his head emerged,

he said, "I used to work for a firm providing private security services to international clients. Most of what I did was protecting infrastructure—dams, bridges, that kind of thing, either employed directly by various governments or working for utility or oil companies. That's also where I know Keegan from, by the way."

"He was a security contractor too? Or, no ... you said he was an engineer. Which is still pretty hard to imagine."

"Yeah, I worked with a crew protecting bridges and things, while Keegan was the guy building 'em. Or doing the surveying and design, anyway. He was a really outdoorsy guy then, the kind of guy with a calculator in his pocket and a gun on his hip. One part brainiac, one part Indiana Jones. He liked working on his own in remote and sometimes dangerous places. I was surprised he came back home and became a cop, but I guess you never know what's going to float someone's canoe."

"And what about Ghost? I'm going to guess *he* didn't work with you. Or did he? No—if you were protecting bridges, I bet he was the guy blowing them up."

"Got it in one." Derek checked his gun and re-holstered it, then offered a hand and helped her up off the log. "I'm not gonna say everything I did was always the kind of thing your mom would approve of. My company got me the jobs, and I went where they told me and did what needed doing. But mostly, I was a guard. A protector. Ghost, on the other hand, was the kind of person who'd get hired by insurgents to blow things up. He was a sort of a professional agent provocateur for hire."

"And you fought." She slipped her hand into his. It seemed so unreal, speaking of battles in far-off places when they were walking in this sunlit forest, serenaded with birdsongs.

"We fought. We clashed a few different times. The last

time I saw him was a few years ago, in the Andes Mountains in Peru. We nearly killed each other."

"That's how you got the scars?"

Derek nodded. "After that, Ghost went to ground, or at least he went off to bother someone else for awhile. I wondered if he might be dead. But I was getting out of the game by that point, too. Decided to come back to the States, started working as a security guard and bodyguard rather than the quasi-military stuff I'd been doing. I hadn't even really thought about Ghost in years, until he turned up in town."

Gaby shivered. "I just want him gone."

"Well, hopefully some of the stuff he's been up to lately will put him away for a good long time. He's wanted in a few different countries, but as far as I know, he wasn't wanted *here*—until now. I'm sure Keegan's already in the process of putting together a case against him."

"Good." She leaned into his side. "I don't really wish him ill. I mean, I don't hope he'd *die* or anything. I just don't want him to bother us anymore. Prison is where he belongs."

So I can go home.

Home ... with Derek? She didn't even have to ask the question. She wasn't sure how they'd fit another person into her small apartment, but they'd have to work something out. She couldn't even imagine her life without him in it now.

She gave a soft laugh.

"What?" Derek asked, and she realized it must seem strange to him that she was laughing now, when they'd just been talking about Ghost a moment earlier.

"Oh, just thinking about life. My life. Our lives. I can't believe we've known each other for such a short time. It feels so natural and comfortable to be with you. I can't imagine *not* having you in my life."

"That's because you're my mate," Derek said. "The one person in the world for me."

She'd heard people talk about soulmates before, but the way he said it—he sounded so *convinced*. Like he was discussing something that wasn't mere philosophy, but a matter of scientific fact.

"You sound so sure of that."

"I am sure. We're always sure. There's only one person in the world for us, Gaby, and you're the one."

She didn't want to intrude on the warmth of this rare private time by bringing up cruel reality, but ... "I thought that about Sandy's father, for awhile. At least I thought I did."

Though ... had she? Looking back on it, she'd never gotten that feeling of comfort and meant-to-be with Sandy's father. She'd been caught up in the whirlwind of a young woman in love, but there had been warning signs from the very beginning. She'd been aware of them even then.

"It's a shifter thing," Derek explained. "That's something we haven't really talked about yet. We each have a mate, one person in all the world who is exactly right for us. The other half of our soul. We're drawn to them. And you're the one for me, Gaby. I knew it the moment I saw you."

Gaby turned that over in her head. It didn't seem possible, and yet, that was exactly what it felt like. She couldn't deny that feeling of perfect rightness whenever she was with him.

"Does it work that way for humans, too?"

"I don't know," Derek said. "I only know about being a shifter. What do *you* think?"

"I think ..." She leaned her head against him. "I think I knew the minute I saw you that you were the one for me; I just didn't want to admit it yet. I don't know if every human has a soulmate, a mate, whatever you want to call it. But I know for sure that *I* do."

DEREK

Keegan called in early afternoon on the land line. "Settling in okay?"

Derek was temporarily alone in the living room. Luisa was lying down for a nap, and Gaby had taken Sandy down behind the cabin to show him the spring, while Derek watched them out the window.

"This place is really something, man. I can see why you like it up here."

"Glad you think so. My dad and I built that place after I came back from South America. Sometimes you just need to get out in the woods and let the animal run, you know?"

"I know exactly what you mean." Through the open window, he heard the sound of a child's cries, and for an instant his heart lurched. He leaned forward so he could see Sandy and Gaby, reassuring himself that the squeals were happy ones. Even though there had been no sight or sound that anyone had followed them, and every reason to believe they were safe here, he wasn't about to stop being vigilant.

"Everything okay so far?" Keegan asked. "No sign of Ghost?"

"Everything's fine, except all you left us to eat is boxes of crackers and pancake mix. Someone's gonna have to make a supply run sooner or later."

"Hey," Keegan scoffed. "I wasn't expecting visitors. Anyway, there's a whole crate of MREs in the storage space under the cabin, and I've seen you live on those for months."

"Maybe *I* can, but I'm not going to expect Gaby to, let alone the old lady and the kid."

Keegan snorted. "There's a little town down the mountain where you can go for supplies. Just be—"

"—discreet, yeah, I know how to do the job, man. So what's the news? Sooner you guys catch Ghost, the sooner I can get Gaby back to her life."

He felt exposed as soon as the words left his mouth; he should have said *get back to* my *life*. But that wasn't what he cared about. What *was* his life, anyway, except some part-time security gigs and a daily workout routine? He didn't even have a pet goldfish.

It was Gaby who deserved to be safe, happy, and free.

"He's either gone to ground somewhere close to home, or he's off looking for you guys," Keegan said. "Let's hope for the first option, especially since Ms. Diaz ran him over with your car. Do you have any idea how badly she managed to hurt him?"

"I couldn't tell. She landed a good hit, enough to knock him off me. His healing ability will still take care of it eventually. I'm confident she didn't hurt him badly enough to kill him. He was trying to get up as we drove away."

"With any luck, it'll slow him down if you do have to fight him," Keegan said. "We did pick up his partner on the armored-car heist. Like I said earlier, he's doing muscle work for a local crime family, and as far as I can tell, that's *all* it is. Just bad luck that you two ended up in the same town at the same time. He's not coming after you because his bosses want him to. Actually, they seem happy to cut all ties. It's personal now."

"Wonderful," Derek said. If Ghost was working under orders, then they could lean on the crime lords controlling him. Ghost as a free agent was a lot more alarming.

"And you're confident he didn't follow you?"

"I know how to shake a tail. How about you? What are the odds someone could find out about this cabin?"

"Slim to none," Keegan said. "Like I told you, it's not in my name. There's no paper trail that would lead to me, let alone any reason for anyone to connect it to you. Stay up there as long as you want."

After he hung up, Derek sighed. He ought to feel better about this, but instead he couldn't shake the feeling that he was missing something important.

Maybe it was just that it went against his nature to hole up while the action went on elsewhere. He felt like he ought to be out there helping. He was the kind of guy who got in the middle of a fight, not the kind who went and hid from one. If he was the only person involved, he would've gone looking for Ghost and tracked the bastard down himself.

But he had more than just himself to worry about now. And keeping Gaby safe took priority over anything else.

Gaby came in from outside with a wet and muddy, but giggling, Sandy in tow. "You know, I might not've thought this through," she told Derek with a grin. "Memo: don't let your kid play in the water when you don't have any dry clothes to change him into."

"Didn't you bring some stuff from the apartment?"

"A few things, but they're totally haphazard, whatever I could grab." She helped Sandy take off his muddy shoes at the door, and then picked up the squirming, giggling child and deposited him on the kitchen linoleum. "Now stay there while I find out if there's anything for you to change into."

Derek got another of Keegan's clean T-shirts; they were going to owe the guy laundry and a good cleaning of the cabin by the time they left. Gaby had managed to turn up a pair of spare little-boy shorts in the backpack. "I don't suppose there's a washing machine here?" she asked.

"Sure is. No dryer, though. That's what the line in the backyard is for."

"At least your friend has utilities," Gaby said, toweling off Sandy. "When I saw what the road up here was like, I was worried we were going to be lighting candles and cooking fish on a stick over a campfire."

"Don't knock it 'til you've tried it. Speaking of which, if we want anything for supper other than canned beans and crackers, we'd better make a trip to town for supplies."

"Is that safe?" Gaby asked, looking up at him.

"Long as we don't go around telling everyone where we are. Keegan said there's a little town down the road a ways where we can stock up."

While Gaby went ahead and got Sandy dried off and dressed, Derek went outside and took a walk around the perimeter of the cabin. He stood for a few moments looking off into the woods, scenting the air.

There was nothing here to be alarmed about. But just like the other time at the apartment, his bear seemed to be telling him that something was amiss. Or maybe it wasn't even his bear, just a low-level sense that he'd failed to take everything into account.

He did a quick, routine check of the car, wincing at the damage to the front end from when Gaby had hit Ghost with it earlier. It didn't seem to have caused any structural damage, though; as far as he could tell, the damage was only cosmetic. He tested the pressure in the tires and propped up the hood so he could check the fluids. Working on the car always relaxed him. He did a lot of the maintenance work himself, sometimes with Keegan's help. He'd never done a complete engine rebuild, but he'd always wanted to.

A possible reason for his unease occurred to him. He tended to think of Ghost as all brawn and no brain, but that didn't mean the guy couldn't have a good idea occasionally. What if there was a tracker on the car?

Derek got down on the ground and scoped out the most likely places on the car to plant a tracking device: under the front and rear bumpers, inside the wheel well, on the frame. He didn't find anything. But there were a lot of hiding places on a classic car like this one. And while they were inside Gaby's apartment building, Ghost would've had more than enough time to plant something. Or maybe even earlier, at the coffee shop.

You're being paranoid, he told himself. Still, paranoia had saved his bacon more than once.

Gaby came out on the porch, holding Sandy's hand. "Do you want to leave soon? I'm getting about ready for lunch. We could get a burger or something in town."

Derek straightened up and slammed the hood. "Sure. Is your mom ready to go?"

Gaby shook her head, dark hair bouncing on her shoulders. "She says she'd rather stay here. I think she's really feeling yesterday's activity in her hips, though she won't admit it."

"I don't like splitting us up. Nobody should be left unattended."

But Luisa refused to be budged. "I have my book," she said, holding up a paperback that looked like it came from Keegan's bookshelves. "And I have a nice cup of tea. I will be perfectly fine here. Buy some pork and I'll make us something nice. A man needs meat," she added, glancing at Derek's shoulders.

Derek crossed his arms. "What this man needs is to keep all of you in the same place."

But short of bodily carrying her to the car, there wasn't much he could do. He scribbled his cell number on the back of a gas station receipt. "Here. Cell phones don't work up here at the cabin, but they ought to work in town. Keep the doors locked and if you get the feeling anything's wrong, anything at all, give me a call."

"I will not hesitate to call at a whiff of danger," Luisa promised, and they had to be content with that.

"You said the cabin's safe," Gaby said as she belted Sandy into the Mustang's backseat. "She'll be okay, won't she?"

"I'm sure she will." Derek tried to push down his misgivings, and his frustration; he could see where Gaby got her stubbornness from.

It was nice to have daylight for the drive to town. He hadn't been able to appreciate the scenery in the dark, but it was really lovely now that he could see it. Although summer still had the city firmly in its grip, up here in the mountains the trees and underbrush were starting to show the faintest hints of color among the green: a flash of red here, of gold there. It was going to be a spectacular autumn.

I wonder if I could talk Keegan into letting me bring Gaby out here later this fall, just the two of us. Without Ghost's presence hanging over their heads, he could take Gaby out in the woods, lay her down among the golden fall leaves, take her glorious body in the autumn sunshine ...

"Penny for your thoughts," Gaby murmured.

Derek grinned at her and flicked a meaningful glance into the backseat, where Sandy was occupied with a handheld electronic game. "Probably not a good time to share them. Ask me again later."

She playfully rolled her eyes. "I would complain about

your one-track mind, except I'm really enjoying the track it's on."

After a moment, she shyly held out a hand. Derek closed his bigger hand over it and laced their fingers together.

~

The town was called Autumn Grove, according to the sign on the highway. It was a pretty little town, framed by picturesque mountains in the background, with an old-fashioned downtown that looked like it should be on a postcard. After picking up some groceries at the town's small supermarket and a cooler to stash them in, they got burgers at a café on Main Street, the kind with checked red-and-white tablecloths and a menu chalked on a big board behind the lunch counter.

I really like it here, Derek thought, looking across the table at Gaby helping Sandy put ketchup on his fries. He had always liked being closer to the land than he could get in the city, and it was easy to see himself being happy in a town like this. Maybe build a cabin like Keegan's, or get a little house closer to town. A couple of acres of land ... room to shift, and roam ...

Except his decisions didn't only affect him anymore. He looked away from the window and the view of Main Street and the mountains, to Gaby dabbing ketchup off the front of Sandy's borrowed, oversized T-shirt. Did Gaby want to live in a small town or in the city? Did she want an apartment, a condo, a house?

We haven't talked about any of that yet.

But they would work it out somehow. For years now, he'd been looking for a purpose in life, and he felt as if he'd finally found it. He didn't care where Gaby wanted to live. Wherever she wanted to be was where he wanted to be.

Gaby looked up and noticed him watching. She smiled, a little quirk of her lips that brought out the tiniest of dimples in her cheek. "What?"

He thought about deflecting, but went for honesty instead. "Just thinking that I like this town."

"Me too," Gaby said, grinning wider. She dipped one of her fries in Sandy's pool of ketchup. "Which is something I never thought I'd say. I've lived in big cities all my life. But it's just so quiet and peaceful out here. I could go either way, you know? What about you?"

"Same. I don't mind the city, and there are a lot of great things about it. But my—there's a part of me—" *My bear,* he'd almost said. "—that will always long for the woods."

Sandy only ate half his burger, so Gaby had it wrapped up while Derek paid the bill. He carried Sandy out to the car, ketchup-stained T-shirt and all, with one of the little boy's chubby arms thrown trustingly around his neck.

He had never imagined that this could be his life.

"Do you see anywhere around here that sells clothes?" Gaby asked. "At some point we're gonna run out of Keegan's spare shirts. And Sandy got his shoes wet in the creek this morning."

The best they could find was a small sporting goods store. Gaby balked at the prices, but Derek insisted on paying, and they let Sandy pick out a few things he liked.

"This looks about your size, doesn't it?" Derek asked Gaby, holding up a women's T-shirt in pink camo.

"Pink's not really my color." She wrinkled her nose at him when he held it up against her chest. "Derek, letting you buy clothes for Sandy is one thing, but buying stuff for me—"

"—is something I'm more than happy to do. Let me treat you." He tossed the pink shirt into their basket. "Pink camo it is."

"Oh, for—" Gaby reached to snatch it out, then hesitated.

115

"Well, my mom might like that. Derek, are you *sure* you don't mind?"

"Pick out a few things for each of you. Gaby, please believe me. I don't mind at all. I've got a savings account that's just sitting there, not doing anything except stacking up interest." He kissed her, slow and lingering, enjoying the taste of her sweet lips. "You've been taking care of everyone for years. Let someone take care of you for awhile."

They walked out with bags full of their purchases, Sandy chattering happily and clinging to his mother's hand. Derek had also picked up a kid-sized fishing pole, because he wanted to find out if there were fish in the creek, and he'd seen some fishing tackle back at the cabin.

Gaby giggled.

"What?" Derek asked her.

She nodded back toward the store. "I think the clerk thought we were a family. I mean, he thought you were Sandy's dad."

"Oh," Derek said, startled. He looked back at the store. "Do you mind? I mean, I could have set him straight—"

"Only if *you* mind," she said, somewhat shyly.

"Hell—uh, heck no. Not at all. I ..."

He wasn't really sure what he was feeling, honestly. It was a warm feeling that welled up from deep inside him, satisfying to both Derek and his bear.

Maybe this was what belonging felt like.

"Mr. Derek?" Sandy asked.

"Yeah, kid?"

"Are you dating my mom?"

Derek looked at Gaby. She ducked his gaze, her brown skin darkening as she flushed.

"I'd ask your mom, kid."

"Mom?" Sandy said, tipping his head back. "Are you dating Mr. Derek?"

"Yeah, hon," she said, her flush deepening. "I think I am."

Derek held out his hand. Gaby slipped her fingers into it.

They walked back to the car like that, hand in hand in hand.

Sandy was tired out, almost starting to nod off, as Gaby buckled him in. Derek looked forward to getting back to the cabin, settling in, locking all the doors, and having a quiet evening in relative safety. Still, there was that nagging sense that something wasn't right.

"Have you called your mom?"

Gaby nodded. "Right before we ate lunch. Everything was fine; she was just reading her book. Do you want me to try again?"

"No, I'm just being overly cautious, I think."

He twisted the key in the ignition. The car roared to life, along with a sudden, startling rattle from under the hood. Gaby jumped.

"Well, that doesn't sound good," she said as Derek hastily reached for the ignition key.

"No, it sure doesn't." He paused before he turned it off. The rattle had been short-lived, and now the engine had settled down to its usual smooth purr. Derek couldn't think what would make a noise like that, when the engine had been running just fine yesterday and this morning. Something jolted loose on the rough road, maybe? A rock thrown up into the engine somewhere?

He shut it off, got out, and looked under the hood, while Gaby craned out the passenger-side door. Nothing was visibly wrong. Derek tested some connections with his fingertips, leaned over to look over the cylinders and fan belt. The nice thing about an old car like this was that every-thing was out there where you could see it; unlike a modern car's engine, it wasn't a densely packed mass of hoses and electronics. If something had broken loose, he ought to be able to see it.

He crouched down and peered underneath the front end of the car. A glint of metal on the gravel caught his eye immediately. Derek stretched a long arm under the car. Probably just a dropped earring or a loose bolt or something, hopefully not anything that would be difficult to replace in a small town like this—

As soon as he got it out into the light, his stomach dropped about ten feet.

"What?" Gaby asked, seeing his face.

Derek turned it over in his fingers, a little piece of metal and plastic about half the size of a credit card.

He'd looked for a tracking device earlier. He just hadn't looked hard enough.

They were making the things so goddamn small these days. That asshole must have crawled under the car and stuck it all the way up inside the engine, where he'd have had to tear apart the whole engine to find it.

And he probably never *would* have found it, if not for two trips over that rough road knocking it loose.

"Gaby, you got bars on your phone? Call the cabin."

The urgency in his voice silenced any objections she might have made. She punched in the number and held the phone to her ear while Derek opened the hood and took a quick look over the engine for anything else visible, any sign of more bugs or sabotage. He didn't see anything—but that didn't mean it wasn't there.

There could be a tiny hole in the brake line, wearing out slowly, waiting to snap.

There could be another tracker, hidden even better.

"It's just ringing," Gaby reported. "No answer."

"Get Sandy," Derek said. "I'm going to need you to—"

And there he stopped, because there was nowhere safe to leave them.

Ghost knew where they were. He knew all their movements. He knew they'd been in town all afternoon.

Every instinct screamed at him not to take his mate into danger -- especially with her cub, who he had started to think of as *his* cub as well. But there was simply nothing else to do. What was he going to do, push her out at the side of the road? Take the time to drive around town and find a motel, when it was always possible that he hadn't found the only bug on the car, and Ghost might follow her there anyway?

No choice.

And, with Luisa in deadly danger, no time.

There was no way Ghost wasn't in these mountains already. He'd had the better part of a day and night to track them down. Derek hadn't smelled him around the cabin— but he wouldn't have. Ghost was a pro, and he knew he was up against a bear shifter. He knew Derek's sense of smell would be as keen as his own. He'd have done exactly what Derek would have done in his place: stayed upwind, watched through binoculars, waited for his chance ...

Such as the rest of them going off and leaving an old woman alone.

No point in kicking himself for it now, though. All they could do was deal with the situation as it stood.

"Derek?" Gaby asked. She was gripping her phone in both hands, staring at him. "What is it? What's wrong?"

"This is a tracker," he told her, holding it up. He dropped it and ground it under his boot heel, feeling the electronics crunch and pop on the gravel.

The blood drained out of her face, leaving her gray. "Mom," she whispered.

"I have to find somewhere safe to leave you and Sandy. Somewhere public, maybe—"

"No!" Gaby shook her head vigorously. "The only place I feel safe is with you. Wherever you leave us, he can find us."

She was horribly right.

"Okay, we're going back to the cabin. You'll stay in the car with Sandy, I'll get Luisa and your stuff, and then we'll get out of here. Okay?"

Gaby nodded wordlessly.

"Mom, what's going on?" Sandy asked anxiously from the backseat.

"Nothing's wrong, honey," Gaby said, taking her seat. Only Derek could see that she was trembling, holding herself in control by sheer force of will. She looked close to tears.

Give her something to do.

"Here." He tossed his phone to her. "I just unlocked it. Look up Keegan and call him while I drive. Tell him everything."

That kept her busy while Derek roared out of town, driving so fast on the rural road that the car was airborne half the time.

He slowed when he turned onto the driveway leading up to the cabin. Ghost, like Derek, had a mercenary background. That meant he knew how to set traps. And if Derek was going to set a trap, this was where he'd do it.

"I've lost reception," Gaby said, her voice faint. "Keegan says he's sending help, but—but it's going to take awhile to get out here."

"Mom?" Sandy asked in a small voice.

"It's okay, honey."

"It'll be fine, bucko," Derek told him, crawling forward over the ruts in the driveway. "Just listen to your mom and do whatever she tells you. Okay?"

"Okay," Sandy whispered.

"Why are you driving so slowly?" Gaby demanded, clutching the door handle as if she planned to jump out of the car and run ahead.

"Making sure the road's okay."

"Why wouldn't the road be okay? We just drove it a couple of hours ago. It's not going to magically not be okay now."

"It would if someone did something to it."

"Oh," she whispered, and fell silent.

Like that. There, ahead of them: a trip wire across the driveway, right at car-bumper height.

No telling what it was attached to—a deadfall, an explosive device, something to puncture the car's tires? He braked hard. The smart thing would be to back the car out to the road, leave Gaby and Sandy in the car, and go in on foot—but he was going to need the car to get Luisa out. She couldn't walk all the way down the driveway, not in her condition.

"What are you doing?" Gaby gasped when he reached for the car door.

"Dismantling a trap. I'm gonna leave the engine running and the doors locked. If anything happens, slide over to the driver's seat, back down the driveway to the road, drive into town, and call Keegan. And stay in the car with the doors locked until Keegan gets there."

She opened her mouth to say something, then closed it and nodded.

Derek drew his gun and got out of the car. He popped the lock down and slammed the door behind him.

The low rumble of the idling engine was the only sound in the very quiet woods.

The one thing in their favor was that Ghost could only be in one place at a time. If he was working with an accomplice, they were screwed.

But Derek still didn't think so. From his conversation

with Keegan earlier, he thought it sounded like Ghost had burned his bridges with his employers in town. Ghost was out here for revenge. He probably hadn't brought any help.

Probably.

Derek walked up to the trip wire carefully, watching the driveway ahead of him. As soon as he got there, he saw that it was a very simple trap. Ghost had cut most of the way through a large tree beside the road. The wire was fastened securely to another tree across the driveway. When the car hit it, the wire would pull down the tree. Depending on how fast they were traveling, it would either crush the car's engine, or fall on the roof and crush the occupants.

Simple. Evil. Deadly.

He got out his pocket multitool, clipped the wire, and kicked it out of the way. The tree swayed a little, but didn't fall. Ghost would have been careful not to cut it so deeply that any errant breeze would push it down.

It was still possible it'd fall and block the driveway before they got back down. He filed that away as a possible hazard for their escape.

Looking back, he saw Gaby watching him through the windshield, eyes wide and anxious. He gave her a thumbs-up and then walked carefully up the driveway, looking around, tense and alert.

He walked just as far as a bend that took him out of sight of the car. If he remembered right, the cabin was around the next bend, and he didn't want to alert Ghost that they'd come back. He found one more trap, a disturbed patch of earth right in one of the tire ruts. Derek brushed away the dirt and found several nails pointed up. He picked them out and threw them into the woods, then retraced his steps to the car.

He tapped on the window and Gaby leaned over to unlock the driver's door for him.

"Are you okay?" she asked anxiously as he got in.

"I'm fine." He put the car in gear and crept forward, speeding up a little as he passed under the deadfall trap before stopping just past the other trap he'd disarmed. The cabin was right ahead, around the next curve. And unfortunately, because Keegan was a paranoid bastard who'd built the place like a fortress, Ghost would have a perfectly nice sniper nest in the cupola up top. Derek wouldn't be surprised if he was already stationed up there, watching the driveway.

This was a terrible place to turn around, but with some careful back-and-forth, crunching into the brush on both sides of the driveway while branches scraped the sides of the car, he managed to do it.

"Aren't we driving up to the cabin?" Gaby asked.

"I need to check it out first. If anything happens—if you hear gunshots, or if I don't come back in, say, half a hour, drive back to town and call Keegan." Derek pointed to his phone, still in her hand. "Put his number in your phone."

"Derek, you can't go fight him alone—"

"That's what I'm good at. You have a more important job. You have to take care of your son."

"I've got the number," Gaby said, handing his phone back. "Still no bars. Derek, I'd feel better if we stayed together."

"So would I, but there's no choice." He patted the steering wheel. "I'm leaving the keys in the ignition. Soon as I get out, slide over to the driver's seat and make sure the door's locked. Don't unlock it except for me."

She nodded, then startled him by throwing her arms around him and planting a passionate kiss on his mouth.

"Ew, Mom, gross!" Sandy said from the backseat.

Gaby caressed Derek's face as she let him go. "Please be careful," she whispered. "Save my mom, and come back to me."

"I will. I promise." He kissed the corner of her mouth. "Take care of your son." He started to reach for the door handle, then looked over the backseat. "Hey, Sandy? Take care of your mom for me."

"Okay," Sandy said solemnly.

Derek got out and slammed the door. Gaby slid over to take his place in the driver's seat as soon as he was out.

She was smart and strong and brave. She'd be okay, he told himself. She'd be okay.

Gun in hand, he walked up the driveway toward the cabin.

DEREK

Right before he turned the bend that would bring him into direct view of the cabin, Derek cut away from the driveway into the woods.

Getting close to the cabin was going to be hard.

Damn it, Keegan, at times like this, it'd be so much more convenient if you were the kind of sloppy homeowner who lets the trees and brush grow right up around the place. Good job keeping it clear. Now there's no way to get close without being seen.

But he could think of one way: the spring. It was in a little ravine with some brush growing alongside it. He would've preferred better cover, but he didn't dare wait for dark.

He circled the cabin in the woods, trying to stay downwind. He wasn't sure if Ghost would be able to smell him from inside, but there was no sense taking chances.

It was quiet enough out here that he could still hear the growl of the Mustang's engine, which meant Ghost could probably hear it too. He'd know they were near. But Derek didn't want to risk having Gaby shut it off. There wasn't a big chance it wouldn't start again—he kept the car in excellent repair—but when their lives depended on it, any risk was too much.

He didn't want to get close enough to be seen, but he took the gamble of peeking out of the woods, between two tree trunks, trying to get a look at the cabin and figure out what he was up against. It looked just like they'd left it. There was no vehicle parked out front. But if Ghost had come through the woods, there wouldn't be.

For an instant, he thought he saw something move in the cupola.

Damn. He was right. Ghost was up there with a sniper rifle. No matter which direction Derek approached from, he'd be seen.

He needed a distraction to give him a chance to sneak up on the cabin. He wished he could get in touch with Gaby and have her do something—but, no, that would draw Ghost's attention in her direction, which was the last thing he wanted right now.

Keegan was sending backup, but it would take hours to get here. Luisa might not be able to wait that long.

Ghost's deadfall trap gave him an idea. Two could play at that game.

He let the woods conceal his view of the cabin again, retreating until he was confident he couldn't be seen. After stripping quickly, he shifted. The strength and energy of his bear surged through him.

He didn't have a chainsaw—but he didn't *need* a chainsaw.

There were a lot of smallish trees around here. Derek picked a likely one, stood on his back legs, and pushed. The tree's roots were no match for the power of his muscular bear shoulders. It tore slowly out of the ground, started to topple, and hung up in the branches of the tree next to it.

Derek shifted and stepped back to look at his handiwork.

The leaning tree was just barely hanging on. It looked like a stiff breeze would send it crashing down.

He didn't bother putting on his clothes. He was probably going to end up shifting again anyway. He picked up his Glock and gave the tree a final shove, making it teeter on its supporting branches.

Then he hurried through the woods on bare, silent human feet. In a few moments he came to the spring, with the trail alongside it that he and Gaby had explored that morning. Derek turned toward the cabin. All the while he strained his ears. When the tree went, it should get Ghost's attention, but his instant of distraction wouldn't last long.

Sunlight up ahead let him know he was getting close to the cabin. Derek stepped into the spring, cool water swirling over his bare feet, and crouched so the bank would hide him from view. He made his way cautiously along the bank to the point where the trail from the cabin came down to the water's edge. If he put his head up, he'd only be a few yards from the back of the cabin—and easily visible from up top.

A breeze swirled over him and rattled the bushes. *Come on,* Derek thought impatiently. *Blow over, you damn tree.*

He'd told Gaby to leave in half an hour. Derek's time sense told him that only a few minutes had passed, but each additional minute crawled by at glacial speed as he crouched with twigs prickling his bare skin, tense as a coiled spring.

Then came the sound he'd been waiting for, the welcome crackle of branches breaking in the woods—he was so on edge by now that even expecting it, he still jumped—followed by the tremendous crash of a tree going over.

Derek jumped over the edge of the bank and dashed for the cabin.

He was only exposed for a few seconds, but every instant he expected to feel the hot graze of a bullet. None came. He reached the back of the cabin and ducked below the nearest windowsill.

The cupola offered a commanding view of the surrounding woods and the clearing surrounding the cabin, but its blind spot was straight down, where the roof blocked the view. Derek figured that he had a few feet around the cabin in every direction where he could move unseen.

He listened for a minute and, hearing nothing, straightened up enough to take a quick peek into the cabin. This was the window through which he'd watched Gaby and Sandy playing in the spring this morning. He caught a glimpse of the living room, looking just like it had when they'd left. No sign of Luisa, though she might be lying down on the couch, tied up and out of his view.

He ducked again and moved stealthily along the cabin wall to the next window, which belonged to one of the bedrooms. It was an opening window, cracked open a few inches to let in a breeze. Derek did the same maneuver, listening and then straightening up for a glance inside.

This time, he hit the jackpot. Luisa was tied up on the bed.

Anger surged through him. She was only an old woman with bad hips. Seeing her lying helpless on the bed, with her hands tied behind her and a handkerchief knotted around her mouth as a gag, sent his protective instincts towards Gaby's family surging into overdrive.

But she didn't look like she'd been hurt. He saw no bruises on her face. Her eyes were open, and she turned her head suddenly, having glimpsed Derek moving at the window.

Derek held his finger to his lips. Luisa nodded.

The window was the crank-opening kind, with a screen over it. Derek carefully and quietly popped the screen out of its frame and lowered it to the ground. Then he tried to work his hand inside to reach the crank. It wasn't open far enough; he couldn't get his hand that far inside.

As a bear, he could rip it right out of the wall, but that'd bring Ghost down in a hurry.

Movement on the bed made him look over at Luisa. She'd struggled to a sitting position, then swung her bound-together legs off the bed.

Derek shook his head at her. She'd not only risk getting hurt if she fell, but Ghost would hear it and come to investigate.

Luisa shook her head back at him, and very carefully, resting her back against the nightstand and then the wall, she shuffled over to the window.

Derek pointed to the crank and whispered, "Can you reach it?"

Luisa shuffled cautiously over to it. Immediately Derek could see that she wasn't going to be able to. She was short, and it was too high to reach with her hands bound at that awkward angle behind her back. When she tried to bend forward to get her hands higher, she nearly overbalanced and toppled on her face. Derek caught his breath and gripped the edge of the window, prepared to shift and rip it open in case he had to come in fighting, but Luisa managed to recover her balance and leaned against the wall, looking shaken.

Derek pointed to her hands and beckoned her to him.

She still looked shaky, but he saw her face firm up with determination—it was such a characteristic Gaby-like expression—and she shuffled over to the open corner of the window. Derek pushed his hand through the gap between the window and its frame, but again, he couldn't reach. Her hands were too far down to untie.

And his knife was back in the woods with his clothes.

Well, there was another option.

"Luisa," he whispered. "Close your eyes. Stand still. And whatever happens, *don't make a sound.*"

The look she gave him over his shoulder was perplexed, but she obediently screwed her eyes shut.

Derek shifted.

The world seemed suddenly smaller, the window flimsier. His bear wanted to fight. It didn't understand all this sneaking around.

First we get the hostage out, Derek told it firmly. *Then we fight.*

His bear was okay with that. It wanted Luisa safe, too.

Derek hooked the edge of his massive paw into the gap between the window and its frame. The window groaned in protest as he carefully snagged the rope with two huge, scimitar-curved claws. It took a couple of tugs and he winced as he saw the rope bite into Luisa's wrists, but then the rope snapped under his claws' sharp edge.

Better than a knife ... at least for some things.

Derek shifted back, his claws shrinking to human fingers curled over the window's edge. He looked up—and straight into Luisa's startled, dark eyes as she looked over her shoulder at him.

"I told you not to look!" he whispered. If she panicked, he'd not only have Ghost to deal with, but also a civilian who would be equally terrified of both of them.

Luisa flexed her hands and untied the gag, making a face as she pulled it out of her mouth. "Ugh. Much better. Are you a bear who turns into a man, or a man who turns into a bear?"

"Uh ... the second one."

"I'm glad to hear that. *Much* better for my daughter." She cranked the window, opening it as wide as it would go. Derek climbed inside. "Are Gaby and Alejo all right?"

"They're fine. They're waiting in my car, down the road a ways."

"Oh, thank God." She looked at him thoughtfully. "I assume that it is easier to turn into a bear with no clothes on."

"Right," he said, and before that line of discussion could go any further: "Where's Ghost?"

"Upstairs." Luisa pointed to the ceiling.

"Does he have a gun?"

She nodded. "A very large rifle."

As expected. Ghost's sniper skills had always been sharp. "Okay, what you need to do is get to the car, while I distract Ghost. I'm guessing you can't run."

Luisa sighed. "When I was a girl, I won every footrace. Now, I can't even walk down the street without my daughter nagging me about using my walker."

"Look at it this way: you couldn't outrun a bear anyway." Or a bullet.

Her eyes went wide. "This Ghost is like you? A bear-man?"

"Yes. He's the polar bear you saw earlier, at your apartment building." As she sucked in her breath to speak, Derek shook his head. "Save it for later. Right now we need to get out. Do you think you can make it from the cabin to the edge of the woods without using your walker? On this uneven ground, it'd probably slow you down."

"I will," Luisa said.

And she would, too. He was *definitely* seeing where Gaby got her grit from.

"Okay," he said softly. "Stay with me."

Gun in hand, with Luisa limping at his heels, he ventured out into the living room to the point where he could get a look up into the loft. There was no sign of Ghost. He had to be up in the cupola.

Leaning close to Luisa, Derek murmured, "As soon as I start up the stairs, go out the door onto the porch, wait for a count of ten, then head for the woods. Gaby is waiting for you in the driveway, right around the corner. Don't stop or turn back for anything."

Luisa nodded without speaking.

Once he'd seen Luisa start for the door, Derek went up the stairs, stealthy in his bare feet, counting under his breath. At ten, Luisa would head across the yard. At ten, Ghost needed to be distracted.

Nine ...

Derek threw the door open and flung himself into the upstairs bedroom. "Hey! Asshole!"

The rifle crashed.

GABY

"**I** spy, with my little eye ..."

"Mom," Sandy whined, squirming in the backseat. "This game sucks. I don't want to be here."

Me neither, honey, she thought. "Why don't you play with your game for awhile?" she asked, twisting around in the seat to hand him the electronic game she'd shoved into the backpack, back at the apartment.

Sandy kicked at her seat instead. By now they'd been sitting around long enough that his anxiety, caught like contagion from the adults, had faded into the fractious boredom of an energetic five-year-old forced to sit in a car with nothing to do. At least trying to keep him entertained gave Gaby something to do. Otherwise she'd be going out of her mind.

Mom ... Derek ...

But she couldn't show her fear. She had to stay calm for Sandy.

"Do you want to draw? I bet I have a pencil in my purse. Let's see if we can find something for you draw on."

"I don't want to draw." Sandy slid down in his seat until he was nearly horizontal and halfway out of the seatbelt. "I want to go home."

And that was what it really came down to, she thought. He'd been having fun on this new adventure, but now he was ready for it to stop.

Me too, kid. Me too.

"How about—" she began, and broke off abruptly at the distant crack of a rifle shot.

"Mama?" Sandy asked. He didn't seem to have noticed it. He was used to a lot of background noise, cars backfiring and distant sirens, the music of the city. The only thing he noticed was her alarm. "Mama, what's wrong?"

"Nothing's wrong, baby," she said through stiff lips, struggling to control her fear. "Everything's okay." She undid her own seatbelt and leaned over the back of the seat to pull the straps of Sandy's belt back into alignment. "Sit up straight, okay? We might have to leave in a minute. You know you have to sit up straight when you're wearing a big-boy seatbelt."

Derek ... Mama ... please, God, please keep them safe ...

She'd just dropped back into her seat and was reaching for her own belt when a movement up ahead caught her attention. She jerked her hand away from the belt and dropped it to the gearshift. The engine was still rumbling as it idled. All she had to do was throw it into reverse.

No, wait ...

"Mama," she gasped, threw the door open. "Sandy, stay in the car!"

Luisa was limping badly, but moving fast. Gaby met her halfway, throwing her arms around her mother and squeezing her desperately. "Mama, thank God, thank God." She looked behind Luisa, but saw no one. Then another distant gunshot made her jump, followed by the quick snap of several more.

"He's back at the cabin," her mother said. "He saved me. He is a good man, Gabriella."

She knew that; oh, she knew that. And now he was fighting Ghost alone.

In that instant, Gaby knew what she had to do. She needed to get her family to safety, but she couldn't leave him alone. She *couldn't*.

"Mama, do you think you can drive Derek's car, with your hips the way they are?"

"When I was pregnant with you, dear heart, I walked two miles to the bus stop every day, and spent sixteen hours a day on my feet, cleaning houses and taking my secretary classes in the evening—"

"So, yes, then. Mama, take the car. Sandy's in the backseat. Drive to town, and call Lieutenant Keegan. His number is in my phone."

"I can't leave you—"

"Yes, you can, you must. Keep Sandy safe. I have to help Derek."

Luisa cupped Gaby's face briefly in her cool hands. "My brave girl. I will not fight you on this. I know how it is with you and Derek. So it was with your father and me. I would have walked through fire for him." She kissed Gaby on the cheek. "Go, quickly."

Gaby helped her mother into the car and then backed away. Luisa hesitated. Gaby waved both arms in a "Go!" gesture. Her mother blew her a kiss over the back of the driver's seat, and put the car in gear.

Gaby watched until the taillights vanished. They were safe. Now she had to make sure that Derek was.

She walked swiftly up the driveway, clenching and unclenching her empty hands. If only she'd thought to check the car for weapons. A tire iron, maybe?

As if a tire iron would do anything against a bear.

As if you *could do anything against a bear.*

But ... maybe she could help. She had an advantage: Ghost wouldn't know she was there.

As soon as she turned the corner up ahead, she could see the cabin in front of her, across an expanse of lawn. She hadn't realized they were this close to it.

There was movement up in the cupola. Gaby remembered being up there with Derek last night. In the dark, there was nothing much to see, but by daylight, you'd be able to see the driveway and anyone coming down it.

That's probably where he is.

Gaby's whole body was knotted with fear, her hands clutched into fists. She jumped when the rifle boomed again, and then twice more, coming from inside the cabin. The fight was still going on. She wasn't too late. Still, self-doubt beat at her. What if she wasn't a help, only a liability?

But no matter what Derek told her to do, she couldn't run off and leave him in danger. They were a team now. He'd stepped up to help fight her battles. She wasn't going to abandon him to fight *his* battles alone.

She took a deep breath, steeled herself, and ran across the lawn.

At any moment, she expected to be shot, but no one shot at her. Derek must be keeping Ghost distracted inside. Gaby reached the porch and relaxed a little now that the porch roof shielded her from being seen. She crept up the steps and cautiously peeked inside the half-open cabin door.

The living room and kitchen still looked just the same as when they'd left, the sink with its drying rack of breakfast dishes, the living room with a few scattered books pulled off the shelves. The doors to both downstairs bedrooms stood open, as did the upstairs bedroom door. With the loft-style upstairs, anyone who emerged from that door would be able to see Gaby in the living room.

She wished desperately that she had a gun.

The uncluttered living room offered few options for weapons. The best thing Gaby could see was a poker hanging on the wall beside the fireplace. It was that or a frying pan from the kitchen. She gripped the poker and tried a test swing. In her hands, the poker that had looked so long and heavy on the wall seemed impossibly flimsy.

Hitting a bear that size with this *is going to be about as useful as trying to beat him up with a Nerf bat.*

But she was committed now. She refused to leave Derek to fight alone.

Cautiously, gripping the poker, she began to climb the stairs.

DEREK

G host's first shot blew a hole in the door, inches from Derek's shoulder. The polar-bear shifter was leaning down through the trap door, awkwardly trying to shoot through the opening.

Ghost fired again, missing in the other direction this time because of the difficult angle, and Derek snapped off a couple of quick shots at him. Ghost jerked back with a hoarse yelp. Derek couldn't tell if he'd hit him or not.

He needed to keep Ghost's attention on him, not on whatever was happening in the yard, where he could only hope Luisa had managed to make it to the shelter of the trees.

Aiming in the general direction of where he thought Ghost was, he fired a couple of shots into the ceiling. The bullets weren't high-powered enough to penetrate the thick wooden ceiling all the way through to Ghost, but there was another startled yelp from above.

"Come down here and fight like a bear, asshole!"

"I prefer having the high ground," Ghost's taunting voice

came down through the trap door. "Seem to recall that worked out pretty well for me before."

They'd fought on a mountainside. Derek remembered Ghost leaping onto him from a boulder, huge claws scoring his side, leaving trails of fiery pain ...

"Fine, you can stay up there 'til the cops get here. You know they're on their way, right?"

"I'll just pick them off as they arrive."

"You're trapped, man. If you turn yourself in, all you have to deal with is a rap sheet for assault and attempted murder. Kill a cop, and you're never seeing the light of day."

"Trapped, am I?" Ghost fired through the trap door, again and again, until the rifle clicked empty. There was the sudden click and clatter of reloading.

Derek shifted to his grizzly immediately, dropping his gun, and swatted the ladder to the loft with one tremendous paw, knocking it down. Now Ghost really *was* trapped.

Derek's bear snarled inside him. It didn't want Ghost to surrender. It wanted a rematch for their fight. Growling, Derek reared on his back legs and clawed at the edge of the framed-in cupola entrance. As he thrust his head and shoulders through the opening, he glimpsed Ghost (still human-shaped) aiming the rifle at his face, and dropped quickly to all fours. The rifle boomed, ripping a hole in the bedroom floor, next to Derek's paw.

They were really wrecking Keegan's cabin. Derek himself had gouged huge slashes in the wood around the opening to the cupola.

But he could no longer hear the distant rumble of the Mustang's engine, which meant Luisa and Gaby had made their getaway. It was just him and Ghost now.

He heard scuffling noises from above. There was a pause and a sudden crash, followed by more scuffling which gave way to an ominous silence.

What the hell was that bastard up to now?

The cupola was completely silent. Derek gripped his gun in his teeth and reared up on his back legs.

The cupola was silent because it was empty. Ghost had smashed out one of the windows; the afternoon breeze washed over Derek's bear nose, bringing him Ghost's scent very strongly.

Bastard's on the roof!

But he couldn't get more than his bear's head through the opening. He couldn't see much, other than a floor's-eye view of the cupola.

Derek hooked a giant paw over each side of the opening, and shifted. Now he was dangling from his hands. He pulled himself up and quickly crouched, looking around.

He couldn't see Ghost on the roof either. What the hell? He'd gone over the side?

A soft noise from below—the bedroom door swinging a little wider—sent him on high alert. He crouched, gun in hand, and leaned cautiously down to peer through the opening in the floor, expecting to see Ghost in the bedroom.

Instead he saw Gaby looking in through the bedroom door, gripping a poker.

What in the hell was *she* doing here? He'd thought she, Sandy, and Luisa would be long gone by now.

The movement up at ceiling height caught her attention. She looked up, wide-eyed. Derek lowered the gun and waved her back, mouthing "Out! Go!"

Ghost was still around here somewhere. Derek *could not* let him get his hands on Gaby.

Looking worried but not panicked, Gaby backed out of the bedroom and disappeared from Derek's field of view.

Where in the hell was Ghost? He wasn't on the roof; he wasn't in the cupola. There just weren't many places to go—

Except one.

Derek looked up at the underside of the cupola's low roof.

The temptation was very strong to just leave him up there. But Ghost on the roof, with a sniper rifle, could shoot anyone who tried to cross the yard. Derek and Gaby would be trapped in the house. Ghost could kill Keegan and anyone else who tried to come help them.

Derek pointed the Glock at the underside of the cupola's roof and fired twice in different spots. He wasn't sure if the ammo was a high enough caliber to penetrate the roof, but it ought to get the attention of anyone up top.

He heard sudden scuffling on the roof. Yep. Asshole was above him.

Fury seized him.

Derek shifted, dropping the gun. As a bear, he nearly filled the cupola. He reared up, throwing his powerful shoulders against the underside of the roof. The whole house shook.

The cupola's roof wasn't meant to withstand heavy loads. A bear, even a large bear, couldn't possibly take the roof off a house, not with a normal roof's support structure of trusses and beams. But the cupola roof was simple frame construction. Everything began to splinter, coming apart. The roof started lifting up at the edge.

There was a thump and Ghost, in his blond-haired human shape, appeared suddenly in Derek's field of view. He'd jumped off the cupola roof and was now crouching on the sloping roof of the cabin, one hand flung out to stop himself from sliding as he balanced the rifle across his knees to point at Derek.

Derek roared and threw himself at the cupola's windows. Frames splintered and glass shattered and half a ton of furious grizzly bear came crashing through the side of the destroyed cupola on top of Ghost.

Ghost managed to get off one wild shot. Derek felt the bullet blaze a trail of pain across his shoulder. Then he landed on top of Ghost, just as Ghost started shifting too, ripping out of his clothes.

The rifle, dropped from hands becoming paws, clattered down the roof and vanished over the edge.

Neither of them cared. By now Ghost's shift was complete, his small furry ears plastered to his skull and lips curling back from his teeth as he snarled.

Derek roared. Finally, he and his bear were in perfect agreement.

You wanted a rematch, asshole? Here you go!

He buried his teeth in Ghost's fur. Ghost tore him with huge, clawed paws. They whirled around each other on the roof, snapping and snarling, locked together in a dance of fanged death. Shingles went flying, ripped out by their claws.

Both of them were too caught up in the fight to even remember where they were until, tearing at each other with teeth and claws, they rolled off the edge of the roof.

GABY

I t sounded like demolitions were happening up on the
roof.

Gaby peeked into the bedroom, clutching the poker.
The first thing she saw was Derek's gun. He must have
dropped it, and it had fallen from the cupola onto the
bedroom floor.

Gaby darted forward and picked it up. It was still warm
from Derek's hand.

The terrific thumping and crashing up on the roof
stopped very suddenly, and then she heard a *whump!* from
down below on the cabin's lawn.

They must have fallen off.

Derek! No!

Gaby looked out the bedroom window, terrified of what
she'd see.

Derek and Ghost were picking themselves up, one brown
grizzly, one yellowish-white polar bear. Ghost's pale fur was
matted with blood. It looked like there was blood on Derek's
fur too, though it didn't show up as well.

The two bears circled each other, snarling. Derek was

limping badly. It looked like he'd hurt his leg when he fell. And Ghost was definitely bigger. He was *huge*, as big as a truck.

How could she change the odds in Derek's favor? She had to do something.

She cranked open the window. There was a screen in the way, and Gaby hesitated for only an instant before punching her fist through it. *Sorry, Keegan. Guess we owe you a new window screen on top of everything else.* She aimed the gun out the gap, carefully lining it up just as Derek had taught her.

Her hands trembled. Looking down the gun's barrel at the circling brown and white bodies made her realize how much risk there was of hitting Derek if she missed.

So don't miss, she told herself, steadying her right hand with her left.

Then Ghost lunged at Derek, and suddenly the two separate furry bodies were a thrashing mass of brown and white on the ground. Gaby tried to follow their fight with the muzzle of the gun, but quickly realized that she didn't dare try to shoot Ghost now, with the two of them so close together. They were thrashing around on the grass, first one on top, then the other.

Before she could decide what to do, they vanished out of sight under the edge of the roof. She could still hear them, snarling and roaring and occasionally thumping into the wall, making the house shake.

Her own lack of fear surprised her. She wasn't scared for herself at all. She was only afraid for Derek.

Somehow, she had to help. And she couldn't do it from up here.

She pulled the gun in, and left the bedroom, running down the stairs.

On the ground floor, the noise of the bear fight was terrifying. The cabin shuddered every time they rolled into the wall. It sounded like they were killing each other out there.

Holding the gun in front of her, she went out onto the porch. Derek and Ghost's snarling sounded even louder out here, without the cabin walls in the way.

She wasn't afraid that Derek would hurt her. Even in his fury, she knew that he wouldn't.

No, her worse fear was that in trying to help, she'd become a liability—a hostage.

But she wouldn't just stand by and let Ghost kill her mate.

She rounded the corner cautiously, but the bears were fighting behind the cabin now, so she couldn't see them yet. The wall of the cabin was scored with huge gouges where their claws had dug into the wood, raw and pale against the weathered brown logs.

Imagine what those claws could do to a person ...

She peeked around the corner at the back of the cabin. There they were.

It looked like Derek might be winning; he had Ghost down on the ground with his jaws on Ghost's throat. But even as she thought it, Ghost swatted Derek with an enormous paw and knocked him sprawling.

Instead of lunging for Derek, he went a different way instead. Gaby thought at first that he was running to escape. Then he shifted back to a man, and his fingers closed over something lying in the grass.

He stood up and turned around with the rifle in his hands.

DEREK

erek started to get up to continue the fight, then froze at the sight of the rifle pointing at him.

Blood streamed down Ghost's naked, human body from dozens of bite marks and claw gouges, but he aimed the rifle at Derek with ruthlessly steady hands.

"Doesn't matter if you're a bear or a human at this distance," Ghost growled. "A bullet to the head will stop you just the same."

Derek shifted too. His head spun with the change from bear to man, but it was easier to think and plan in his human shape, and he really needed that right now. He gauged the distance between himself and Ghost, but it was no good; he didn't think he could make it without getting shot.

"Nothing to say for yourself?" Ghost demanded.

"Just that it didn't have to be like this." Derek wiped blood off his mouth with the back of his hand. *Come on, Keegan, get here already. What's taking you so long?* "We were both just doing our jobs. It never had to be personal. And for me, it never would've been, if you hadn't gone after my mate."

"Always the self-righteous bastard, weren't you? Taking

146

you out as a bear would've been satisfying, but I'm glad I got to look into your eyes before I—"

The sound of a gunshot drowned out his words.

But it wasn't the deafening crash of the rifle. Instead it was the sharp report of a pistol.

Ghost jerked.

Gaby stood less than twenty feet behind him, Derek's Glock gripped in both of her shaking hands.

Derek didn't think Gaby had managed to hit Ghost anywhere vital. He wasn't collapsing; instead he started to turn around.

And Derek leaped forward, shifting as he went.

He slammed Ghost to the ground and whacked him hard in the head with one big paw. Shifting human again, he slugged Ghost hard in the jaw and then smacked his head on the ground until he stopped struggling.

"Gaby, quick!" Derek called. Gaby blinked, snapping out of her temporary paralysis. "We need something to tie him up, something strong. Chains or a really heavy rope. Check the outbuildings."

Gaby nodded and took off running. Derek kept most of his weight on Ghost. When his captive started to stir, he slugged him again.

Gaby came running back. "I found this. Will it work?"

It was a steel winch cable on a spool. "Perfect," Derek said grimly. "Hold one end for me."

He didn't have anything to cut the cable with, but that would probably work okay. He wound it around Ghost's wrists and feet, and knotted it tightly around his body, until Ghost was trussed as securely as Derek could make him.

When he stood up, his leg nearly collapsed under him. It felt like he'd twisted an ankle, probably when he fell, but with the adrenaline coursing through his body, he hadn't even noticed.

"Bring the guns," he told Gaby.

She picked up the rifle and carried it awkwardly while Derek, limping, dragged Ghost around to the front of the cabin. The support posts for the porch were the most secure thing Derek could think of to tie him to. He knotted the winch cable tightly around two of the posts, leaving Ghost slumped between them, wound in several yards of cable.

"Will that hold him?" Gaby asked anxiously.

"It better. He's not strong enough to break a steel cable—trust me, I should know—so if he tries to shift like that, he'll cut his hands off. That ought to hold him until the police get here."

Gaby nodded. Her lips trembled, and her face was ashen. "Is it ... over?"

"It's over. It's over, honey."

Derek gathered her into his arms, pulling her against him. She threw her arms around him, heedless of the dirt and blood. She was trembling all over.

"You did good," Derek said into her hair.

"I shot him," she gasped. "I shot a man, oh God, I shot a man."

"You didn't kill him." He'd seen the bullet wound when he was tying up Ghost. She'd winged him across the shoulder blade. "You just grazed him. He'll be healed by tomorrow. But you distracted him. Kept him from killing me. Gaby, you saved my life."

Gaby buried her face in his shoulder. "I don't know why I'm such a mess about this," she said, slightly muffled. "I wasn't scared at all while it was going on. And then it just hit me. I don't know why."

"That's how it goes sometimes. I've been there. And I've seen big, strong, combat-trained guys who didn't behave as well as you did under pressure." He kissed the top of her head. "Did I say you did good? I should have said you did *amazing*."

Gaby laughed shakily. "So, uh ... where are your clothes? Did you rip out of them like the Hulk?"

Derek couldn't help laughing. "No, I planned ahead. They're in the woods. I can tell you where, if you'll get them for me. Cable or no cable, we probably shouldn't leave this guy unattended."

He sat on the porch with the rifle across his knees while Gaby retrieved his clothes from the woods and then went into the house to look for first-aid supplies. When she came out, she was laughing, with a slightly hysterical edge to it. "Keegan's cabin is a total wreck. I bet he's never having *you* over again."

"Hey, we can always blame this jerk." Derek pointed at Ghost with the muzzle of the rifle.

"Turn around so I can patch you up." Gaby started swabbing at his lacerations with a warm, wet cloth. "Aren't you going to need a hospital for all of this? Antibiotics and things?"

"I'll be fine. You saw how fast the other bite healed. But I'd like to get as much of this as possible covered up before the cops get here, in case Keegan brought regular human cops as well as shifter ones. I don't want any awkward questions."

"So it's a big secret, right?" Gaby asked, dipping the cloth in the red-swirled water. "The shifter thing."

"As much of a secret as we can make it." Derek tried not to wince. He was enjoying his mate's ministrations, but now that the adrenaline from the fight was wearing off, he felt every scrape, bite, and bruise. "Shifters like Keegan—cops, doctors, government officials—try to make sure that the real facts of a situation like this don't get into the reports. That way, ordinary shifters with families can go on living their lives."

"So it's not like some kind of organized conspiracy, like a government cover-up."

Derek shook his head. "Not really. It's more just that shifters work together to make sure the human world doesn't find out about us. Individual humans, sure. A lot of us have human friends, allies ..."

"Mates," she whispered, kissing him lightly.

"Yeah," he murmured into her warm, soft lips.

She let him go and went back to swabbing at his injuries. "Don't worry. Your secret is safe with me. It's going to be hard to keep it from my family, but—"

"Actually, you don't have to. Your mom knows. She saw me shift while I was rescuing her earlier."

"Oh." Her eyes went briefly wide. "Er, how did she take it?"

"Fine. The only questions she asked me had to do with making sure I was going to be a good mate for you."

"Of course she did." Gaby sighed, but her smile was very fond. "I'm sure she'll have plenty of questions later on, just to warn you."

"It's a price I'll have to pay." He smiled before turning serious. "We probably should wait a couple of years before telling Sandy, to make sure he's old enough to understand about keeping the secret."

"Yeah, we still haven't broken the news to him about Santa Claus. Probably better to hold off a little while on revealing that the Easter Bunny might be a guy who *turns into* a bunny."

"If he is, I've never met him."

Gaby laughed softly and bent her head over his arm, gently disinfecting a parallel series of claw marks across his forearm.

Derek looked down at the dark, tousled top of her head. It still felt so unreal, not just to have found his mate, but also an entire family to go along with her. He never would have expected to feel so welcomed by a group of humans.

Even after they knew what he was.

His sharp ears caught a sound. "What?" Gaby asked, looking up quickly when she felt him tense.

"Engines. Sounds like cars coming up the road. Let me get my shirt on. You can go dispose of that stuff."

Gaby dropped the cloth into the red-tinted water. "If there are regular cops, aren't they going to wonder why Ghost is stark naked and looks like he got mauled by a bear, too?"

"Good point. Bring a blanket while you're at it."

He'd just gotten finished putting on his shirt and throwing a blanket over Ghost's huddled form when a state trooper vehicle pulled into the yard. Keegan was out almost before the wheels stopped turning.

"Late to the party, as always," Derek called, straightening up stiffly.

"What'd you do to my cabin, man?" Keegan demanded, looking up at the ruined cupola. "This is friendship?"

"Hey, we got you a present to make up for it."

Keegan lifted the corner of the blanket and flashed a quick grin. "He's alive?"

"Still kicking. He's either genuinely unconscious or faking it." Derek nudged him with a toe. "Anyway, I guess I don't have to tell you to be careful with this guy."

"Don't worry, we've got reinforced cuffs in the car." Keegan jerked his head toward the troopers who were getting equipment out of the back. "They're friends of mine. They know about us. And how are you doing, ma'am?"

"I'm okay," Gaby said. "What about my mom and my son? Have you seen them?"

"They're in town, with a car full of state troopers to stand guard. At this point I can probably tell them to stand down. It doesn't look like Ghost is working with anyone anymore."

"You said he was working for one of the local crime families." Derek put an arm around Gaby, pulling her closer to him. "Any chance they might send someone else after her?"

Keegan shook his head. "Unlikely. Ghost's very public revenge crusade is exactly the kind of publicity they don't want. At this point, they're very happy to cut all ties with him. We've got the other perp from the armed robbery in custody, and it looks like things are going to end there."

"I can go home?" Gaby asked hesitantly.

Keegan smiled at her. "Yeah. You can go home."

Derek sat back down on the porch steps, Gaby at his side, and watched as the troopers cuffed Ghost hand and foot, before cutting him out of the winch cable with a pair of wire cutters Keegan produced from somewhere around the cabin.

"The phone's not working either," Gaby told Keegan. "I think Ghost sabotaged it somehow. What's his real name, by the way?"

"Still working on finding that out. Don't worry, we'll have a name to charge him under soon enough."

Gaby rested her head on Derek's shoulder.

"Holding up okay?" he murmured to her, once Keegan and the troopers were no longer in earshot.

"Tired," she said, and gave a sudden, soft laugh. "And thinking about how we ran away from our apartment building and left dinner on the table. There's going to be a mess to clean up when we get back. Um ... there *is* an apartment to go back to, right?"

Keegan returned just in time to overhear this. "Your apartment building's fine. Well, mostly fine. There's some smoke damage on the first floor, but you should be able to move right back in."

"If you want to," Derek told Gaby quietly.

She looked up at him, eyes wide and bright. "What are you thinking?"

"I'm thinking your place isn't very big, and neither is mine. When your lease is up, I think maybe we should look for somewhere with a little more space. Enough bedrooms nobody has to share."

"Unless somebody *wants* to," she said teasingly, pressing her cheek against his shoulder. "Do you think we might be able to find a place with a yard for Sandy to play in?"

"I think that sounds perfect."

Gaby laced her fingers through his. With her warm, soft weight pressed against him, he felt her giggle again. He knew what she was feeling; relaxing tension often turned into giddy relief, when even the tiniest things seemed unendurably funny.

"What are you thinking about?" he asked her quietly.

"I was just thinking that, with Ghost caught, I guess teaching you to run the espresso machine was completely pointless. You'll never have to draw another shot of coffee, unless you just want to."

"Only if we open our own coffee shop."

He expected her to laugh, but instead she was quiet in a thoughtful kind of way.

"Is running a coffee shop something you want to do?" he asked after a moment.

"Is that weird? You know, I've thought about it. I would like to own my own business someday. I'd always thought it was something I never *could* do ... startup costs and property rental in the city would've killed me. I had to be practical for Sandy and my mom's sake. But ..." She hesitated, working her thumb in slow sweeps across the back of his hand. "Ever since we've been out here, I've been thinking about how many of the things I used to think were impossible actually *could* be possible if we thought about moving somewhere with lower property costs. I bet I could open a café in a little town like this for a fraction of what it'd cost in the city. Of course, there'd also be a smaller customer base. It would never be a wild success." She looked up at him. "I'm sorry. I'm rambling. And anyway ... I don't think you'd *want* to live in a small town, would you? I didn't think I would. Except, the longer we've been out here, the more I like it."

"I'm actually more comfortable in rural places," Derek admitted. "It's the bear in me. I've mostly stayed in the city because ... actually, you know, I'm not really sure why. Inertia, I guess. It's easier to find work there, but it's not like I couldn't get a job somewhere more rural. The kind of thing I do, I could do just about anywhere."

Her laugh—God, he was starting to love that laugh—came out on a huffed sigh of relief. "I'm so glad it's not just me. I guess I just bonded with this little town as soon as I set foot in it. There hasn't really been time to think, and I know this isn't a good time to be making decisions about our future, but ..."

"No need to make any decisions right away," Derek told her gently. "Especially not 'til all this is sorted out. We have time."

"Yes." She gripped her fingers tightly around his hand, interwoven with his. "All the time in the world."

"This is perfect," Gaby declared.

She knew she'd probably been saying that every five minutes for the entire time they'd been looking at the house, based on Derek's fondly amused grins every time it slipped out again, but, well, it *was* perfect.

It was spring now, and ever since their adventure in Keegan's cabin the previous summer, she'd had a mental picture of the kind of place she wanted to live in. As the winter had gone on, as her relationship with Derek deepened and grew until the commute between their separate apartments had started to feel like the distance from the Earth to the Moon, she'd added detail after detail to the dream house in her head.

And this place was probably about as close as she was ever going to get, at least not without costing so much that it priced them right out of Derek's savings.

It was just outside the same little town where Keegan's cabin was. She'd loved the cabin, but she didn't want something quite *that* remote, especially with a child who was starting first grade this fall. But this was close enough that

Sandy would be able to walk to school, and Gaby could walk to the little downtown where she had already noticed a perfect ground-floor retail space with a FOR RENT sign in the window.

The house was on three acres with an old horse barn and an overgrown pasture with a stream running through it. There was a fireplace in the living room, a gorgeous master bedroom upstairs (with windows looking out on the woods), a bedroom for Sandy, and another for the sister he was going to have in the fall. Gaby touched her pregnant belly lightly as they walked from room to room.

There was even a little guest cottage across the yard that she knew her mother would absolutely love, so Luisa could stay nearby while also having her own space.

No more Mama in my kitchen. At least not constantly. I love her, I really do, but .... enough is enough.

And it had a price tag she simply couldn't believe. You wouldn't even be able to get a condo in town for a price like this.

She reminded herself that the cheaper cost of houses in the country came with drawbacks, like fewer jobs and fewer customers for the coffee shop she was already dreaming about.

"I think that's the look of a woman in love," the real estate agent said, ticking off a mark on her clipboard.

"It sure is," Derek said, sliding his hand around her waist. "We're getting married this summer."

"I think she meant with the house, dear," Gaby said, tilting her head back to smile saucily up at him.

"... oh."

"But that too," she added, standing on tiptoe to kiss his nose. "What do you think? I mean, I don't want you to feel like I'm making the decision for both of us. If you don't like it—"

"Are you kidding? I love it. There's plenty of room in the woods to—" Aware of the real estate agent's presence, he amended whatever he was going to say to, "—ramble, as much as we want. There's space for a woodshop and workout area in the old barn, and ... did you have the same thought about Luisa moving into the guest cabin?"

Gaby nodded. "It's—"

"—perfect," Derek finished for her, and swept her into a dip and a long, lingering kiss.

Hours later, with the initial round of paperwork done and the gears set in motion on the long purchase process, they left the real estate agent's office and wandered around the little downtown, peeking into antique and hardware stores. Sandy was with Luisa in the city, and Derek and Gaby made it clear that they wouldn't be back tonight. It felt strange and luxurious to Gaby, having the whole afternoon just for the two of them.

"Knowing you," Derek said, squeezing her hand, "you've already got your coffee shop location picked out."

"I sure do. Right around this corner."

She stopped in front of the picture window with the FOR RENT sign. It looked like it had been awhile since this little brick building had had a tenant; the glass was dingy, and last fall's dead leaves were drifted in the doorway.

But that just meant it might be possible to get a good deal on it. And then she could make it her own. She could already smell the tantalizing scents of fresh-brewed coffee and baking cinnamon rolls. She was helping Polly in the kitchen at the Daily Bean now, and Polly had given her the responsibility of making the morning donuts, which coming from Polly was the highest honor that could be bestowed on a fellow baker.

This wasn't precisely the use she'd meant to put her business and accounting classes to, or at least not the most lucrative of the possible options. But after all this time working at minimum wage for someone else, the idea of owning her own business, being her own boss, thrilled her to her core.

"Here we go again," Derek murmured, kissing the top of her head. "You've even got a name picked out for the business, don't you?"

"I'm thinking we can call it the Brown Bear. Where the coffee is 'as strong as a bear.'" She made air quotes.

Derek burst into laughter. He sounded joyous and free. For all the changes Derek had wrought in Gaby's life, she was endlessly grateful to have been able to give him something meaningful in return. He was almost a different person now, playful and happy, a devoted father to Sandy (who had started calling him "Dad") and in all ways a much happier and more contented man than when she'd met him.

"As long as you don't want me to pose for your sign."

Gaby grinned and put her finger to her lips in mock thought. "That's a really great idea. Thanks for suggesting it."

"Me and my big mouth—"

"Hey there, you two! If it isn't the last two people I expected to see."

Gaby didn't recognize the man waving at them from the opposite sidewalk until he jogged across the street to join them. She'd only ever seen Keegan in his sharply dressed police lieutenant persona, but this was obviously Keegan in country-cabin mode. He was wearing a plaid shirt, rolled up at the sleeves, and jeans.

"Hi, Gaby," Keegan greeted her, and to Derek, "I'm surprised you're willing to show your face in town, after what you did to my cabin."

"Hey, man, haven't I been coming out on the weekends to help you fix it up?" Derek put an arm around Gaby. "Anyway, that's no way to talk to your newest neighbors."

Keegan let out a laugh and slapped Derek on the shoulder. "You actually did it. You're buying a house here."

"Just put in an offer today." Derek pointed down the street. "It's right outside town. Gorgeous place on three acres. I think Gaby's already arranging the furniture and redoing the wallpaper in her head."

"Shows how much attention *you* were paying," Gaby said, whapping him gently in the arm. "I'm not a wallpaper kind of girl. In fact, the first thing we're doing is stripping that awful wallpaper in the living room so it doesn't overwhelm the pretty wooden molding on the shelves."

"See what I mean?" Derek said, winking at Keegan.

Gaby snorted. "Mm-hmm, and I heard you making plans to completely remodel the barn, so this sounds like a case of pot and kettle to me."

"That's amazing," Keegan said. "You two even *sound* like a married couple. When's the wedding, again?"

"June," Derek said, "and you'd better be there, because it's tough to have a wedding without the best man."

"I assumed my invitation got lost in the mail."

"We haven't sent out invitations because we were hoping to have the wedding in the yard of our new house," Gaby said. "Except the house-hunting process has been going pretty slowly. I think we've finally got it, but we're obviously a ways out from closing."

"You're missing the perfect solution," Keegan said. "You can have the wedding at my cabin. I don't mind, and I know you two both loved it up there." He paused, frowning. "Assuming you want to. If you don't want to get married on a spot where you almost died, I get it."

"Actually, I think it'd be a good way to erase those memories and replace them with new, better ones," Gaby said slowly. She'd had her heart set on getting married in her very own yard ... but now that she thought about it, their new house was probably going to be chaos for the first few months as they moved in and worked on the various remodeling projects they'd planned. Adding the chaos of a wedding would be a bit much.

"Gaby?" Derek asked. "I'm happy with whatever you want. The only ingredient I really need for the wedding is you."

She squeezed his hand, and leaned forward to plant a kiss on Keegan's cheek. "It's beautiful up there. We'd love to. Thank you."

And now that she thought about it, she could picture a gorgeous ceremony beside the creek, the lacy skirt of her white dress rippling in the wind, the woods making a perfect scenic backdrop to the ceremony ...

"Uh-oh, I know that look," Derek said cheerfully to Keegan. "She's probably got the ceremony halfway planned out in her head already. Have you written my vows yet, hon?"

"Are you kidding?" she asked, twining her fingers in his. "I wrote our vows months ago. Why put off something that important until the last minute?"

"Right, all you're putting off are the unimportant things, like the actual location of the wedding."

"Hey, we have one of those now, thanks to—um." She paused and looked curiously at Keegan. "I don't think I've ever heard Derek say your first name."

Keegan laughed. "Really? Well, in *that* case, I think I'll just stay mysterious for now. Most people call me Keegan anyway."

"All you have to do is look it up on the police department website," Derek told her.

"Spoilsport," Keegan said. "Anyway, since we seem to be straying onto the topic of the police anyway, I did want to tell you two that a verdict was handed down on Sorenson yesterday."

It took Gaby a moment to remember that Sorenson, as it

turned out, was Ghost's real name. She would probably always think of him as Ghost.

"They're putting him away for a good long while, I hope," Derek growled, tightening his arm around Gaby.

"You better believe it. We've managed to not only get him for his attacks on the two of you, but also for several mob-related killings elsewhere in the country. You won't be seeing him again anytime soon."

"Oh, thank God." Gaby sagged against Derek. Even knowing Ghost was behind bars, there had been a part of her still struggling with the knowledge that he was still out there. Some nights she woke from nightmares of a polar bear trying to tear its way through her door, rolling over to touch Derek and reassure herself that she was safe.

But now he'd be going away to a maximum security prison.

It's over. Really over, this time.

"You okay?" Derek murmured into her hair.

"I'm fine," she said, and was surprised to realize she meant it. "For the first time in months, I really feel like everything is gonna be okay."

"Well, in that case," Keegan said, "let me treat you two to a burger in the finest small-town diner in Autumn Grove. We like to welcome new neighbors around here."

As they turned to walk down the street in the fresh, warm spring afternoon, Gaby looked up at the mountains. They held no fear for her now, nothing but a sense of promise and beginnings. She had a new life with Derek to look forward to, and she couldn't wait to get to it.

If you'd like to read more about Derek, Gaby, and Keegan,
Bodyguard Shifters continues in
Pet Rescue Panther!

What's hotter than a sexy man holding an adorable kitten?
How about a sexy, protective panther shifter cop holding five
adorable kittens! Ben must protect curvy cat-rescue
volunteer Tessa (and her box of kittens) from the dragon
assassin who has sworn to kill her.

Now available on Amazon and Kindle Unlimited!

A NOTE FROM ZOE CHANT

Thank you for buying my book! I hope you enjoyed it. If you'd like to be emailed when I release my next book, please click here to be added to my mailing list: http://www.zoechant.com/join-my-mailing-list/. You can also visit my webpage at zoechant.com or follow me on Facebook or Twitter. You are also invited to join my VIP Readers Group on Facebook!

Please consider reviewing *Bearista*, even if you only write a line or two. I appreciate all reviews, whether positive or negative.

Cover art: © Can Stock Photo Inc.

ALSO BY ZOE CHANT

Bodyguard Shifters

Bearista

Pet Rescue Panther

Bear in a Bookshop

Day Care Dragon

Bull in a Tea Shop

There is a convenient boxed set of the first four books.

Bears of Pinerock County

Sheriff Bear

Bad Boy Bear

Alpha Rancher Bear

Mountain Guardian Bear

Hired Bear

A Pinerock Christmas

Boxed Set #1 (collects Books 1-3)

Boxed Set #2 (collects Books 4-6)

And more ... see my website for a full list at zoechant.com!

If you enjoyed this book, you might also like my paranormal romance and sci-fi romance written as Lauren Esker!

Shifter Agents

Handcuffed to the Bear

Guard Wolf

Dragon's Luck

Tiger in the Hot Zone

Shifter Agents Boxed Set #1

(Collecting *Handcuffed to the Bear, Guard Wolf,* and *Dragon's Luck)*

Standalone Paranormal Romance

Wolf in Sheep's Clothing

Keeping Her Pride

Warriors of Galatea

Metal Wolf

Metal Dragon

Metal Pirate (forthcoming)

Metal Gladiator (forthcoming)